About the author

Born in Halifax, Nova Scotia, I grew up travelling the globe extensively as 'military police issue'. Often being entertained with crime stories by my father's circle of friends and inspired by their delightful, twisted tales, I quickly became a fan of mystery thrillers. A lifetime later, staring at the greatest mystery of all, suddenly I was sixty-seven and married forty-five of them with three children and eight grandchildren. So, now for amusement, along with family and writing more of those offbeat whodunits, I'm a musician/songwriter and—between chapter, song and verse—walk about forty miles a week to keep the mystery alive…

FIVE DAYS IN MAY

md newcombe

FIVE DAYS IN MAY

Vanguard Press

A CIP catalogue record for this title is
available from the British Library.

ISBN 978 1 784658 35 9

*Vanguard Press is an imprint of
Pegasus Elliot MacKenzie Publishers Ltd.*
www.pegasuspublishers.com

First Published in 2020

**Vanguard Press
Sheraton House Castle Park
Cambridge England**

Printed & Bound in Great Britain

Dedication

To family and friends,
past and present

Part I

Chapter 1

Sometimes what you least expect is just what makes life interesting, like opportunity knocking. If you're lucky, it'll only knock you for a loop. Then again, it could knock the door completely off its hinges as everything blows up in your face, trigger a sudden turn of events, an unsuspecting chain reaction and the last day of the rest of your life. Interesting...

—MAY 6TH, CRACK OF DAWN—

"Rise and shine, lover-boy," said a gunman from just inside the doorway to Lannigan's bedroom. "Get your ass out from under that blonde and make it snappy! Turns out, you've got a pressing appointment this morning with a mutual friend." He paused, sniggering. "Well maybe friend isn't *quite* the right word. Now let's go! I don't have all day, mister-got-me-some," added the tall, heavy set, dark-haired goon, seething with testosterone down to knuckles that looked like they might need to be combed and drawing nearer to the couple along with a second man—a silent shadow—following his lead.

"What about the girl?" asked Lannigan. "She has nothing to do with this, whatever it is." He wavered briefly; considering the possibilities, though, he did exactly as he was told.

Slipping from the sheets, he stood up wearing nothing but a puzzled look and a tattoo on his shoulder, eyeing the two pugs ogling the voluptuous young woman kneeling on the mattress, attempting to hide the remainder of her charms and wrapped tightly in a white, linen toga. She gazed up at the man wielding the weapon, about to speak.

"*Whatever*, I really don't care. It's you he wants, one way or the other. And to tell you the truth, it makes no never-mind to me which," replied the gunman, continuing to study the blonde beauty hypnotized by the six-inch, stainless steel shaft of his revolver and, at the same time, reaching over and tossing Mick Lannigan his pants hanging off the end of the bed. "Only, for God's sake—and mine—put something on," he grumbled, glancing around the tiny quarters and then quickly back at the private eye stepping into the trousers he grabbed from next to the bed. "That lily-white skin of yours is blinding me, hard-ass. No doubt the kind of skin that burns from standing in front of the fridge-light too long. You Irish are all the same," he declared, laughing and looking away momentarily, detecting an empty holster draped over the top of the cluttered bureau and, all at once, made nervous by the discovery.

Playing a hunch, knowing the man's reputation as well as the neighbourhood, he redirected his attention, spotting a pistol poking its ugly head out from beneath a pillow. The gunman smiled while nudging his shadow with an elbow.

"You just might want to work on your bedside manner," suggested Lannigan, adjusting his belt while still looking around for his other shoe.

"You just might want to work on shuttin' *the hell* up! Or likely as not, shootin' off your mouth will become my speciality, haha! And just so no one gets any funny ideas, my friend will take that popgun next to you there, Blondie," he ordered, waving his own piece like a pointer as the distraught female reached for the detective's Colt. "Come on, hurry it up, Sherlock. Before I lose my patience altogether and before you lose far more than that pretty little *fucking* wench of yours." He grinned, jerking the gun in his hand and accentuating his raw demeanour.

Watching his silent partner being handed the misplaced, ivory-handled .45, he became distracted, hearing a horn blare from the other side of a window. He suddenly noticed a cockroach scurry across the floor and disappear as the half-dressed and, obviously, not-so-private dick snatched a wrinkled shirt from the brass headboard and started to put it on…

Mick Lannigan lived in a tenement row in the heart of Ledbury, barely beating some said. But nothing special to be sure; in fact, he'd recommend to his prospective clients that it might be safer to climb the fire escape than walk through the lobby to get to his office-apartment at 2261 Palladin. It was on the second floor by elevator, at the end of an abandoned hall, if you were willing to even make the effort and take the chance. Though he always knew, much like life itself, the location and his situation, were only temporary. One day you're down and the next you're on top of the world. The difference is no more than a clean break. Whether that was somebody's neck, an arm, several fingers or perhaps a lucrative case would fall victim to luck-of-the-draw just like it usually did. Still, eventually the odds would swing in his favour, he mused, if he could hang onto a healthy roster of body parts. Then, with the perfect blonde draped over his arm and the right case in his back pocket, he'd be set. Somewhere across town on easy street where they kept all the good bits life had to offer, and on the other side of the tracks for a change.

When he wasn't roaming the dingy streets of the world just outside, that's where you'd find him doing what he did best–no, not that. Well that too apparently as long as she was blonde, but he was a detective according to all the clues, at least for the time being. To be honest, it wasn't his first choice and it probably wouldn't be his last. He was just good at it. Like rats are good at finding crumbs or dogs digging for a bone. Like gamblers at finding ways to win or another way not to lose. No offence to Mick Lannigan, but yes, even like those *goddamn* lawyers and shyster politicians he hated and despised so much that would tell you just what you wanted to hear. Just long enough to blind you from the truth and sway your focus, and all of it just to get the goods or in Mick's case, his next paycheck.

He was every bit the huckster, audacious, hard as nails, rough around the edges, incorrigible to the core and convincing when he was supposed to be, having learned a long time ago how to sell himself. The man had a way of making blind people see his point. He never claimed to be subtle and you couldn't miss it, blind or otherwise. He kept just about everything he needed under his hat except for a piece of luck he strapped next to his heart. But when you're a detective, most of those characteristics are considered pluses in a good survivor's manual. Beyond that debatable array of credentials and quirks, he only knew two things for sure about himself.

He wasn't born to wear a suit and he wouldn't die well. Neither really a skill, he realized. Still, the combination and the philosophy pushed him in the right direction from his shabby, little flat on the east side down near the docks, where the air smelled like fish on a good day and week-old road-kill on a bad one.

The shingle on the door of number 222 said, 'Lannigan — Private Investigator. If you made it this far—congratulations—you might as well come in. If there's no one here, do yourself a favour and take the fire escape on the way out… but leave the steps. Thanks, Mick'.

His present address was a bitter pill in anyone's estimation—especially those that had business with the man—directly across from a recent, and most vicious, murder scene. Death by explosion was the verdict reported by local authorities and the reason for sealing off the corridor, along with the stairwell adjacent to it, weeks earlier. Both were condemned, having been obliterated by the blast and the landlord couldn't be bothered after pocketing the insurance settlement. It was only a matter of time before the rest of the building experienced a similar fate, suggested Doris, making the point daily. And that's precisely when you'd find his secretary, Doris Harrington, manning the phones so to speak, daily, and seven days a week, keeping the growing list of creditors at bay and the riff-raff to a minimum.

Today was no exception. However, according to the clock on Mick Lannigan's bedside table, today hadn't started yet. Not for some people anyway. And for others, well, what's a guy to do when he's caught with his pants down, the little hand on the five and the big hand caressing the trigger of a .357 Magnum willing to blow his head off?

Chapter 2

Mick Lannigan considered becoming a lawyer at one point. But then, knowing himself as well as he did, he also realized that it would probably be a waste of time. This night especially the man seemed satisfied his instincts had been correct. He was convinced he'd never be able to pass the bar speaking as judge, would-be-attorney *and* defendant. It wasn't a legal issue, rather one of substance. And his present whereabouts—though not a 'force majeure, fait accompli—was just one more argument supporting that case...

—MAY 5TH, LATE EVENING—

"How's about another, Skully?" suggested Lannigan, hoisting his empty glass in the air before sliding it across the bar to the man in back of it.

"Sure thing, Mick," replied the bartender, drying the lip of a thick, beer stein, hanging it from a shelf behind him in front of a mirror and flipping the well-worn, white towel over his shoulder. "And by the way," he said lowering his voice, beginning to pour the man's choice on the rocks, ironically summing up the unemployed investigator's life, and luck, lately, then reaching across the bar, setting the man's drink in front of him. "You might want to keep an eye on that blonde in the corner. She's sure keeping her pretty eye on you pretty good," he chuckled, watching his one and only customer at the counter consider taking a drink and then quietly, suddenly, put the glass back down to appreciate the reflection instead, a breathtaking vision stealing his focus for the moment.

"I'm way ahead of you, Skully, but thanks for the advice, old friend. He added, "And for the company," toasting his host while continuing to stare at the mirror behind the grey-haired barkeep. "It's not that you're not a, well, a frigging sailor's delight; in fact, in some circles I'm sure you are," kidded the tall, charismatic Irishman. "Still, you're just not my type." He laughed. "Not blonde enough maybe. So why don't you set up a wine-spritzer for the young lady over there who *is*, in say oh, I don't know, a couple of minutes," suggested Lannigan before downing his two fingers of Napoleon brandy. "And another one of these puppies for me," he winked, turning and beginning to walk towards the stunning, well-dressed woman sitting alone at the back of the bar. Mick nonchalantly adjusted his fedora, front to back and then back to the front again, stylishly tipped to one side, topping off his open trench coat.

"Good evening. I couldn't help but notice you're all by yourself back here," he declared, sharing an affable smile. "A man would have to be blind or even dead not to, I imagine," he said, quickly regretting the remark as he remembered the news that morning and took his hands out of the pockets of his coat.

She responded with a smile, sultry and sweet, still only listening, though enjoying his natural swagger.

"I mean, you don't need to be a detective to spot a missing person," Mick stumbled, temporarily sidetracked and losing his train of thought, thankfully and gently derailed by the beauty gazing up at him. Completely beguiled by the woman and regardless of the consequences, familiar telltale clues or the fact that he struggled to rub two thoughts together at that precise instant, he was set to tempt fate once more. "Anyway, I just don't think someone as attractive as you should ever be in a situation like that," explained the wide-eyed admirer. "Alone that is. So I'm here, compelled by conscience I suppose, to thwart this despicable curse keeping you company. And if your wish is to be rescued..." he paused, feeling his heart race like a stallion making the clubhouse turn and heading for the chute, "...then I stand before you, as you will."

"Really," she said under her breath, looking flushed.

"Absolutely," replied the cavalier, reducing the volume in his words. "My valiant steed, admittedly a borrowed beast by unforeseen circumstance, awaits just beyond these castle walls, fair lady. Ready when we take our leave. In the meantime, however, I thought perhaps you'd welcome some stimulating conversation." He teetered, out of ideas and searching for a clever, next line. "I certainly know I would," Mick confessed, smiling awkwardly. "Still, don't judge me by the dialogue so far. I'm always a bit slow out of the gate, but like any seasoned racehorse after riding all those curves, I explode through the straightaway given the right lead and finish up like gangbusters. So what do you say, gorgeous? Do you mind if I…?" He grinned, gesturing to join her, and continued, "…attempt to save you from yourself?"

"Am I to understand you'd be my noble knight? A fearless Prince Charming willing to risk everything and end this fate worse than death?" she asked with a come-hither smile, embracing the occasion.

"Who knows, destiny's a mysterious mistress. When you least expect her, she often deals you exactly what you're looking for even if you're not sure what that is yourself," he proclaimed, all at once realizing the cards he'd been dealt. "In which case, I may be doing *her* and us both a favour. But to answer your question, yes, I am," he replied, undaunted and wrapped up in the role. "A prince by a pauper's paradigm and a poet's pen, fearless to my last breath, having slain dragons by the dozen and demons by the score," he recited, displaying a confident air as Skully arrived with a tray.

"You're very sure of yourself, aren't you, Mr. Lannigan?" she declared, noticing the drinks while her lips took on a sensuous form, teasing his eyes.

"I have no choice. A man in my line of work has to be," he stated, momentarily perplexed hearing his name mentioned. "And as sure as I am, *usually*, sometimes even I'm surprised, like say, now for instance. It seems you have me at somewhat of a disadvantage," he remarked, sitting down, fascinated by her and scarcely detecting the bartender who was delivering their order right on cue.

Eventually, glancing up, Mick passed the man his last twenty-dollar bill, folded over, and feigned his 'Diamond-Jim' facade, suggesting that he keep the change.

Skully obliged the man with little effort, tucking the money in the pouch of his apron.

"I don't recall ever seeing you in here before tonight. Believe me, I pick up on details like yours, or at least I used to once upon a time. And the fact that you know who I am leads me to conclude you were anticipating my arrival at some point this evening. Which also means much of this act is just that, an act. Why all the charades, good-looking?" he asked without missing a beat, instinctively eyeing the room for anything out of the ordinary other than the lady he was presently keeping company.

"I was told I'd find you here if I waited long enough. I had my doubts. Men are about as reliable as a weather forecast in this country. Though as it turns out, you were worth the wait after all," she yielded in soft tones through a silky voice that told him he wanted her to say more than she was willing. But for now, anyway, he was willing to wait around a little longer to hear it as he noticed Skully tidying up a nearby table out of the corner of his eye.

"So is this personal or business then, or is it something else I'm overlooking altogether?" he inquired, briefly gazing over at Skully with a look that said he was looking for a little privacy.

Understanding the message, the barkeep returned to his place behind the counter, whipped the damp dishtowel from his shoulder, grinned and, whistling a familiar tune, began wiping down another glass as two men in suits entered the tavern.

"Now what's it all about, sweetheart, and take your time. Apparently I have all night as long as I don't skip town," reported the shamus, swallowing most of his cocktail in one foul swoop; listening to the ice cubes clink and rattle around inside the glass as if tumbling dice were determining the outcome of the rest of his life, turning it into another kind of crap shoot and suddenly enjoying the exquisite fragrance of her perfume drifting across the table like some seductive drug, affecting more than just his sense of smell.

"Then we already have something in common. So do I," she whispered, breathy and revealing a delicate innocence through a striking shade of red lipstick. "But to answer your question," she said changing her tone completely, "I'm looking for a husband." She admitted as cold as tempered steel on the stainless blade of a butcher's, stained meat cleaver.

"Uh-huh," replied the detective, taking pause and with a furtive glance, noting there was no ring on her finger. "A husband... I see! So much for introductions then, astrological signs or favourite colours," he submitted, half in jest and leaning back in his chair; not really sure what to make of the blonde-femme fatale as she raised the wineglass to her mouth, took a discriminating sip and then, just as cool and calmly, set the drink back down.

"It's Cassandra, but I prefer Cassie, Cassie Carlisle," she offered from a short-lived silence. "And though signs of the zodiac have always mystified me, I do know I'm a Scorpio according to a number of stargazers I've crossed paths with, and most of who were from their own galaxies... far, *far* away. As for colour however, I'm not confused in the least." She lingered deliberately. "It would have to be the exact shade of your eyes, Mick. Bedroom blue with that steely satin glow; yes, it's suddenly my favourite." She desisted, smiling, taking another drink and staring back at him over the rim of her glass.

"Okay I get it," he laughed. "You know who I am so you probably know what I do as well. You know I find things, mostly people and usually alive, so *what* then? You want me to *find* you a husband, is that it?" submitted the man asking the questions, jumping to conclusions based on a bad day that left him dubious at best and giving the woman very little time to reply. "Well here's the thing, sugar… Cassie, is it? I try not to get involved in those kinds of sordid affairs. Sure, business in my neighbourhood may have ground to a halt like a fine powder in the hands of a dead, Winnipeg wheat farmer. And, arguably, I no longer possess the deftness to track down a case, *let alone* a missing person, but I draw the line at marriage counselling and matchmaking. Sorry, sister, you've got the wrong chump this time. I also know that it doesn't look like it right now, but my feet are planted firmly here on earth and not in one of those far off galaxies you referred to," he stated, caught up in a whirligig of his own devices and beginning to feel the effects of his ultimate reason for being in The Mayflower Tavern in the first place. He was disturbed by the idea she initially brought to the table when he joined her and then like a swift, backhanded slap to the face, cooled by her subtle dismissal. All at once he was relieved and yet somehow, at the same time, irked to think that something very promising had been reduced to nothing more than a business arrangement at best and, at that, the worst kind.

"No, it's not like that at all," she confessed, quietly amused by the whole misunderstanding, hijacking his ride on the Mickey-go-round and he, believing she could read his mind. Playing with her drink and twirling the tall, slender stem of the glass between her finger and thumb, she announced, "I want to find one in particular—mine," altering her posture while he did the same. "The one who's been cheating on me faithfully since the day we were married, the two-faced, two-timing low-life slug! And *then* just long enough to wring his neck before I sue his ass for every penny he's got ..." She floundered, rolling back her tone. "Though, I suppose I have a better chance of scooping money out of this wineglass than I will from him, the son-of-a-bitch!"

"Okay, evidently you have some issues with the man. And it sounds like you might be entitled," he acknowledged, all of a sudden nursing his spirits a sip at a time and pondering what sort of clown would brush off a dame like the one sitting across from him, completely captivated by her stunning features and each one, a stroke of genius. "What's the name of this, this fool husband of yours?"

"Antelo Pilattzi, you can't miss him. He's as big as a mountain, strong as an ox and every inch Italian, the double-crossing, little whore-collector!"

"And what makes you think he's waiting around to be found, Ms. Carlisle? By you or anybody else?" he insisted, taking on a more professional manner.

"He was seeing someone, here, in Delray. A little tramp by the name of Adella something or other. That's all I know. Anyway, a friend gave me your name. He said you were good at getting whatever you went after and that, as far as he knew, you were available."

Lannigan started to grin, considering the praise. He was nearly flattered, given the full rendering of the well-intended compliment, but recognized however that if that were true, he wouldn't be sitting where he was, doing what he was doing with another empty drink in his hand and staring across the table at a beautiful blonde, yanking at his heartstrings and scorching his eyes. Then, reassessing its source without too much effort, he curbed his frustration and smiled just the same.

"I need you to help me find him, Mick. I need you to be the knight in shining armour you said you were and slay one more dragon breathing down my neck."

That's curious, he contemplated, listening to her soothing patter, sincere and sullen and even sexy somehow as she reached into her purse for a cigarette. He considered the odds, mindful of the woman's name she'd used as all the memories suddenly came flooding back. 'Adella'—what was the likelihood that a delicious stranger whom he'd never met before, and who could seemingly cast her own mysterious spell over him, would conjure up the name of an ex-girlfriend from his recent history whose hex he was still living under? Destiny truly is a shrewd temptress, he thought, remembering what he'd told her moments earlier.

Digressing, Mick recounted his short and steamy, sometimes serious and always volatile relationship with the twenty-eight-year-old by the same name, Adella, Adella Hughes, in a montage of inescapable flashbacks. Still, that was then and this was now, he resolved, all at once aware of the blonde caressing his face from the other side of the table, studying the cryptic lines running back and forth across his chiselled brow and the incisive thoughts being dragged, kicking and screaming, through each one. All the time thinking he was contemplating her dilemma and what she was asking of him.

Antelo and Adella, the combination alone— reminiscent of a Shakespearean sounding tragedy— wouldn't allow that to work, surely! Not if there was any justice in the world, debated the man and then quickly counted the holes in his present line of thinking. Smiling quietly with his eyes locked on the lady, he was again, misconstrued by her as much more. After reviewing the last day or two, or even months for that matter, in his personal universe, there was no evidence of anything like that. The word had simply lost all meaning.

Justice was a misnomer, a myth like 'true love', 'happily ever after' and 'lady luck' he decided; though, he was somewhat encouraged by it suddenly and desperate to end his relentless string of misfortune. Why not with someone who could make him forget even though the girl was long gone? Dead and buried in a past that unfortunately couldn't be, not yet anyway. Or maybe it was just the drinks doing all the talking. Perhaps it was Napoleon stealing the conversation, and his focus, so convincingly. Either way, Lannigan was prepared to listen to the argument. It just felt right. It had been quite a while since it did but, all that said, the detective was satisfied that justice had nothing to do with it.

"Look, why don't we get out of here and continue this conversation somewhere more secluded, like, say, my place," he suggested. "Still, I should warn you, it's not the penthouse at the Harbour-front Hilton. Far from it as a matter of fact," he professed, showing his precarious, even jaded, frame of mind and determined to trade away his lead in the last leg of the final race of the day at Rideau Carleton.

"I've been to a few tracks and bet on a race or two. Occasionally you just have to pick a thoroughbred you're comfortable with, and then let it ride like you know he will," said Cassie in crescent tones, beginning to admire his vulnerable side and dapper, good looks even more. "I'm willing to take my chances," she murmured beneath a warm, Cheshire smile, stroking his hand and getting up. "Always go with the *dark* horse. Besides, I appreciate your honesty, Mick. It's rare in someone like you," she admitted grabbing her purse off the table. "And like the sign on your door says: 'you've made it this far—Congratulations.' You know the rest, tall, dark and have-some." She grinned, taking hold of his arm while they headed for the exit to Palladin Drive and his valiant steed, a white, '92 Oldsmobile this particular night down in Ledbury.

Not that far up the street from the Mayflower— inside his apartment—Mick Lannigan exploded out of the final curve like he'd promised. Riding the rail down the stretch, he broke away from the rest of the pack and—leaving behind a cloud of dust along with two thugs in Italian silk—made his move for the finish line, already anticipating a daily double...

Chapter 3

It's a common notion that most things happen in threes and when they do, it's never good, not usually anyway. Place your bet. Let it ride and watch another opportunity slip through your fingers as you get rapped on the knuckles or kicked in the teeth. Life's just like that sometimes—in fact a good deal of the time—and there's not a damn thing we can do about it really except suck it up, and then take a seat on the bench when you hear that call strike three...

—MAY 5ᵀᴴ, THAT MORNING—

"Hey, cutie—how's my favourite, brown eyed girl?" said Mick Lannigan, leaving the woman very little chance to respond as usual, still making his way down the corridor. "And is that coffee I smell?" he enquired, shaking off the dregs of another restless night, savouring the aroma and beginning to consider the day's agenda past the bottom of a sturdy cup.

"Every morning for the last two years I've put on a pot of coffee. And every morning you feel the need to act surprised," replied his secretary, sitting at her desk and watching her boss enter the main area of the apartment from a short hallway. The space—converted from a small living-dining room—had two five-drawer highboys doubling as file cabinets containing this and that, from bullets to a half bottle of eight-year-old bourbon and an odd collection of eclectic furniture, including an old hat-rack with an empty shoulder holster hanging from it. There was a pair of white wicker chairs, a weathered sofa, a bookcase, a floor lamp and a long, narrow table the detective used for his own purposes, a catchall where everything would end up. Things like a cigarette pack with a phone number scribbled on the open flap. Several files and loose papers were scattered across its surface, an ivory-handled Colt 45, Rally sunglasses not yet in season next to a wad of crumpled foolscap and something that resembled a ham sandwich; though without proper facilities and a substantial research grant, it was only speculation at best or perhaps a memory game. Beyond that, he really had no clue, no one did.

Rounding out the décor—and the centrepiece of the room near the door leading into and out of the apartment—was a massive wooden desk sharing the limelight with, and belonging to, Doris Harrington.

"Doris, look around you for crying out loud. Look outside. I'm surprised *you* show up every morning." He smiled, pouring a cup of steaming, black coffee into an equally black, Planet Hollywood mug from Nashville.

"Well, it's not *so* bad. I imagine it much like riding the eye of a storm, most days." She giggled. "An endless whirlwind that keeps tugging me back into the fray where I hang on for dear life. Sometimes I feel like one of those stampede rodeo riders or Dorothy in the 'Land of Oz', but with far less attractive scenery and fewer lines to say." She stopped, seeing the late-riser sample her blend that had absolutely no possibility of driving Tim Horton's out of business anytime soon. "I still haven't figured out who you're supposed to be though. Ordinarily I'm torn between the Wicked Witch and the heartless, rusty, old Tin Man. However, more and more lately, you're beginning to resemble the prickly Scarecrow. But either way, if the city's smart, they'll bulldoze this entire block and we'll be forced to move, she said *hopefully*. I'm sure it's what I live for, Mickey," offered the short and shapely assistant, casting a smile and catching his eye. "Oh, and by the way, I haven't heard from your friends down at the fifty-second precinct since I arrived this morning."

"Let's just build on that good fortune, shall we? I couldn't take another frigging fiasco like yesterday, at least not anytime soon. From the second the man opened his mouth till the moment he marched out that door like some goose-stomping fascist mumbling 'don't skip town', it was all a bit well, melodramatic for my taste, him *and* his ridiculous search warrant. If this keeps up, what do you say we go pump gas for a living, 'sweetheart'?" He laughed after doing a pitiful impression of Rick Blaine and willing to accept the accusation. "That lieutenant had all the charm of a reptile salivating over fresh meat. Sure, they have circumstantial evidence. They always do. Besides, they can usually twist opportunity into just about anything, including motive. Given the fact that it's been almost two months now, they're apparently desperate and about as frustrated as a sorry pack of hounds can be after losing the scent. Somebody somewhere has done the math and they're putting the screws to these guys, pretty damn good. Meaning the cops will nail anybody they can to a cross, or a tree for that matter, but they're barking up the wrong one this time," insisted the trenchcoat, prepared to bet his most recent gut hunch. "Chasing shadows is what they do best." He paused. "I had no reason to murder Adella or her male acquaintance that night," said Lannigan, recalling the blonde's last words to him outside her apartment door, directly across from his.

"...Yes, I do, but I'm leaving, Mick. I'm getting out of Delray at the end of the month. It's just better that way. So don't try and stop me, please.' She started to tear, stepping inside without another word. "You know that," he continued. "I couldn't, Doris."

"Well, hon, maybe they don't see it that way. You are the last surviving ex-boyfriend as they say. As good a suspect as any considering your credentials and, according to Lieutenant Stern, your notable penmanship," she remarked in her patented disapproving tone as the telephone rang. Flipping her hair back away from her ear, she answered it before it could ring a second time. "Lannigan Investigations," she announced in her natural, throaty fashion. Listening intently to the caller, Doris glanced over at Mick to see him rifling through his trousers for a set of keys and quickly covered the mouthpiece. "Do you know someone by the name of Runyan?"

"Yeah, Jack, Jack Runyan. You've met him. He's my bookie, on occasion, when I've got some loose change or maybe a fin or two burning a hole in my pocket, why?" he asked, deflecting attention from his poorly contrived defense, watching Doris roll her eyes at his weak recant and well aware of her views on the subject.

"Yeah, whatever you say, Mr. Liar-liar-pants-on-fire," she rhymed off. Then all at once, hearing the reason for the call, the brunette's appearance took an about face, defined by a crestfallen and stoic, pale complexion. She lowered the receiver, leaving her hand over the mouthpiece. "He was killed in an automobile accident around ten o'clock last night near Albion and Airport Road."

"You're kidding, right? He was going to be my first stop," he informed her, shaking his head. Usually its the pony that gets scratched from the race, not the bookie. *Hell*, I could live with that, he mused, disappointed at himself for what he was thinking. "*Son-of-a-bitch*, who *is* that," inquired Lannigan, whispering as if he could be overheard and nervous it might be some kind of trick after everything that had happened with local authorities recently.

"His brother, he's been going through a phone pad of Jack's that he found in his flat," reported Doris, sympathetic and visibly shaken. She shrugged her shoulders, unsure of what to do or say.

"Just find out about the funeral arrangements. Never mind, I'll take it," offered Lannigan, seeing the lifeless expression on her face and reaching across the desk as she passed him the receiver.

"Hello," he began in a sombre tone. "You're Jack's brother then... Daniel," he said, repeating the name, listening to the fellow at the other end and convinced it wasn't the police. "Yes, that's right. Look, I'm sorry to hear about Jack. He never told me that he had a brother, were you close?" asked Lannigan, taken aback by the sudden doubleheader and sitting on the corner of the desk, still reeling from the news.

There was a lengthy silence. "Yes, I can well imagine, it's true," he offered. "You just never know. Do you have any idea about the funeral, when it might be? I suppose not?... *Really*, sure, uh-huh, yeah, I know the place. Jackie mentioned it one time a couple of months back as a matter of fact when someone else I know was ki—" Mick stumbled. "Passed away unexpectedly as well. Anyway, Jack thinks," he said, hesitating briefly. "*Thought* quite highly of the Mother Superior and the Sisters of the Virgin Mary Cathedral. Yes exactly, and thanks for letting me know. Right.

Again, my condolences. Yes I will, bye Dan," he ended, sounding as solemn as when he'd begun, giving up the phone to Doris and not saying anything for the next few minutes.

"Listen, I have to go out for a little while. I need to see a man about a horse." He paused, suddenly pensive and focusing on the life and turbulent times of Adella Hughes. Reminded by a simple word association, 'man-horse-Jack-death-Adella,' and then another, 'dumped-ex-girlfriend-explosion-blonde-doublehomicide-letter-foulplay-apartment—crawling-with-cops—motive-detective-opportunity-suspect-across the hall-Adella Hughes-murder-life-and spending the rest in prison.' "Tell me something, brown-eyes, do you ever feel like your life is being manipulated somehow and that the world is unravelling right in front of you because of it?

"Every *day*," replied the young secretary. "Look around for crying out loud," she quoted him, gathering a smile that at last appeared, but arrived strained, still empathising with Runyan's brother.

"Right," he conceded. "Then I guess I won't bore you with the details, but I almost forgot what it felt like to win, Doris. After a long line of losers, my horse finally shows up at the *right* end of the race for a change. Gingersnap in the fourth thanks to a girl down on the corner at that Adonis Bakery. You know the place I mean? Anyway, it seems I don't need a racing sheet after all, or a tout. I've been doing it all wrong and paying good money for bad tips all this time. As it happens, I just need to eat baked goods more often. And this particular little lady was a longshot riding at, '*kaachiiiing*', forty-to-one," he stated, sensing his smile dissolve along with the extent of his luck. "End of story and twelve hundred large goes south with the dealer. Serious cash I could really use about now." He hesitated. "He did it to me again, Doris." Mick smiled, staring out the window towards Palladin through a crisp May morning, imagining Jack Runyan gazing back and grinning at him for an instant while he snatched the healthy sum of money from his waiting hand once more, and listening to Jack's quintessential response that he'd heard so often over the years when he did, '*kaachiiiing*'.

"Looks like that wave of bad luck is no longer just a ripple, my dear. It's turning into one of those damn tsunamis everyone's talking about and tearing up the coastline and *my life* along with it. Maybe I'll have to move even *farther* inland. As for this coffee, it did the trick. Hot, black and fine as ever, thanks," he said, handing her the empty mug. "And while we're on the subject of bad luck, you might want to consider a new profession, young lady. One that gets you out of here and away from me for a start. I don't know if you've noticed it or not, but people are dropping like flies lately. If not though," Mick continued, grinning, "I'll check back with you around noon. Just in case Delray's finest are out combing the streets for me and my elusive shadow. I'm thoroughly convinced they couldn't track down in a pillow with or without the factory tab, and one of my only regrets is I can't even kick the stupid out of them without it smarting. So if they do call, tell them to stay put. I'll find *them*." He chuckled, putting on his coat. "By then maybe you'll know about that insurance job with Abitibi. So long, Doris," he said before choosing to leave by the fire escape with his coattail flapping in the breeze while the metal landing rattled and rumbled beneath his feet.

From the rear exit, he was able to survey the alley below and except for an adjacent building jutting out on the far corner, he could nearly see where he remembered parking his car—a '95 silver Intrepid—the night before.

Shortly after descending the staircase and reaching the parking lot, Lannigan returned to his office, entering it the same way he'd left, though perhaps his demeanour had deteriorated somewhat between visits.

"Here's a twist of irony, Doris, could you get the police for me? I'd like to report a stolen car—mine," he declared.

"Ahhhh, Mick."

"On top of that, everything I own of any value, except for the .45 over there and a few personal things I keep in the bedroom, was in the trunk," he said, wondering when the next shoe would drop and wishing it was in the four door sedan along with the rest of his life.

"This really isn't one of your better weeks." She paused, looking uneasy, broadcasting more bad news long before it left her lips, while the private eye braced himself for the incoming breaker—a rolling whitecap—listening for a loud, number-nine wingtip to hit the floor with a discouraging splash.

"What," he floundered, faltering and reviewing his growing list of options. "The insurance company called?"

"Sorry, hon, all the artifacts have been recovered. Mr. Nason thought they should let you know right away so you wouldn't miss out on any other situations that might come your way."

"Yeah, certainly my biggest concern of late, beating back potential clients with a baseball bat, and they found *everything*, where?"

"He didn't say, only that they'd turned up and weren't going to be needing your services after all. He did remark however that they'd keep you in mind," she advised him, searching for a positive spin on the day's downward drift.

"*All of it*, Cobb's cleats, the Babe's last Red Sox Jersey?" He hesitated. "The entire collection?"

"He said everything, Mickey. On that, the man was crystal clear," she reiterated, hesitating momentarily. "Though noticeably vague about any of the details," stated Doris, recounting the conversation. "And almost apologetic, I might add."

"Uh-huh, that's amazing, isn't it?" he declared, appearing more sceptical than surprised by the news. "You know, if I didn't know better, and perhaps I don't, I'd say someone was trying to keep me off the streets and unemployed, and doing a damn fine job at it too. Look, after you get hold of the police, you'll have to call Nason back anyway. My car, and that lot stashed away inside, is insured with them. Maybe he can make it up to me," said Lannigan, flopping down in one of the wicker chairs and considering another cup of coffee, the last time he'd had a legitimate case he didn't lose money on and just how much pumping gas might actually pay, full time...

Chapter 4

Bad things happen to good people. Or maybe they only look like bad things masquerading as something completely different, leading to 'God knows what? On the other hand, perhaps those 'good' people are tiptoeing between here and there just pretending to be something *they're* not. And presented with the length of time we rattle around this muddled maze dancing life's journey—to death—the odds are better than good we'll face our share of adversity no matter who we pretend to be scurrying about as. Much like the good book says, 'Shit happens and somebody's going to pay the price'. To paraphrase its author-creator, 'somebody has to'. Call it equal opportunity; call it collective conscience, tough love, comeuppance or just a bad day in the life of Mick Lannigan. But whatever you call it, nasty things still happen to nice people by and by, by and large and forever by the book...

—MAY 4TH, JUST BEFORE NOON—

"Why don't you take a little walk, Miss Harrington; maybe buy yourself a new pair of shoes," Mick suggested, recognizing several of the officers entering his apartment, though not the lieutenant flashing the badge. "My guess is you're not old enough to have this kind of fun, not yet." He winked, flashing a smile at his secretary. Quickly taking her overcoat from the chair, she stood up to leave, understanding the tone in his voice.

"Wise decision," added the senior police detective, watching the brunette make her way to the door past a near naked hat-rack. "Your boss is right. We don't need any witnesses gumming up the works." He laughed, reaching into his jacket before returning his focus to the private eye. "Why don't you have a seat, Mr. Lannigan? I have a few questions." He grinned. "Oh yeah, and this warrant here to search these premises," declared the man with the badge. Flapping the piece of paper back and forth in the suddenly, stale air and then, scouring the room with a reckoning stare, tucking the document away in his side pocket.

"What kind of questions? And about what, *specifically*?" demanded Lannigan as he noticed his secretary stalling by the doorway.

"All in good time," he replied, watching the attractive, young assistant flip her hair back over the collar of her coat. "But I am here for as long as it takes, and till I'm satisfied about some nagging details, and doubts. Between us, I'm convinced we'll get to the bottom of them." He hesitated a moment. "One way or the other," said the lieutenant, leaning comfortably on the edge of the desk, preferring to wait until she was gone and scrutinizing the layout again as Doris issued a furtive glance at the heavy-set officer and then towards her boss, a tall, slender man in contrast.

"Are you going to be okay, Mick?" she murmured, disturbed by the demeanour of the man hovering over him. "Should I call Nesbitt and Finch before I go, just in case?" Her gaze fell on the podgy police officer once more, this time with a visible look of misgiving.

"I'll be fine, brown-eyes," he smiled. "Still, if it comes to that, I'm sure even these fellows will let me make one call. Go on now, scoot! Get out of here," said Lannigan, directing her with a subtle tilt of his head, composed and confident. Reluctantly, she pulled the door closed behind her and stepped out into the hall.

"So what's this all about?" asked Lannigan with a waning lilt in his pitch. "As if I didn't know," he mumbled under his breath.

"Where do I begin..." replied the lieutenant after a lengthy lull, sizing up the man on the couch glaring back at him, "...how about with your landlord?"

"My landlord, what's he got to do with anything?"

"That *is* why we're here, I ran into him. On purpose in fact, just yesterday afternoon revisiting that nasty incident with your ex-neighbour in 221." Lannigan perked up, subconsciously shifting to the edge of his seat. "And even though he's a curious little creature and reminds me of something that climbed out from a Second Avenue sewer, he has a way with words. Yes, sir, Mr. Dunvega passed along all kinds of fascinating tidbits."

"For instance?" asked Lannigan.

"Well, for starters," he said, his eyes wide open, "it would seem that you'd been keeping more than a little time with the now deceased, Adella Hughes in the land of not so long ago or far away. Conveniently across the hall, as it happens. Nice for you, unfortunate for Miss Hughes I have to think, you know, in retrospect."

"Why you mealy-mouthed *son-of-a-bitch*," Mick sniped, leaping to his feet only a short distance from the officer and looking as though he wanted to lash out at the suggestive remark and the man wielding it. But instead, he desisted as the other two officers approached, their hands instinctively clutching for weapons beneath a layer of polyester.

Immediately raising his arms to quell the moment and submitting to the numbers, Lannigan backtracked, slowly stepping away from the lieutenant. "You can imagine whatever you like, it's a free country. But just keep your comments to yourself unless you've got something to back them up or I *will* be calling my lawyer. And while you're at it, why don't you do us all a favour and just crawl back in that gutter alongside Dunvega so you don't contaminate good people with all your snipe and snide, little innuendoes."

"You're a pistol, Lannigan. Shooting off your mouth like an adolescent buffoon and taking pot shots at anything that moves. That tells me plenty, though it doesn't help me much." He paused. "Instead of going off half-cocked, why don't you do yourself a favour and put your trigger-happy tongue back in its cheeky holster and just give it a rest for a bit. You know, one of these days you're going to come up lame and seriously hurt yourself if you keep jumping to conclusions like you do. All I meant was, given the explosion that destroyed her apartment, ah, never mind. Niceties are obviously lost on the likes of you," he professed, shaking his head and rubbing a handful of stocky fingers over a day's worth of dark stubble. "A little testy this morning, aren't we? No one warned me you were playing with a short fuse," declared the lieutenant. "Yes indeed, you are the surly one, and way too jumpy for someone with a clear conscience and nothing to hide, Lannigan."

"I have *nothing* to hide, except maybe a tattoo I'm beginning to regret and, of course, my contempt for police arrogance. It's slime like you that give cops a bad name," he asserted, hiding a smirk and locking eyes with the officer, willing to throw away the key for a while. "It's like I told the other homicide detective, it must be six weeks ago now. 'I was in the shower at the time. I didn't see, *or hear*, anything'! It's not the best alibi, but then as even *you* probably know, the best ones are either already taken or completely choreographed."

"We'll see," replied Lieutenant Stern ignoring much of his response, but unable to look away. "In the meantime, have a seat before I lose my patience altogether. Before I decide to get creative and let these

45

yahoos join our friendly little powwow. Well, I'm waiting, flatfoot. Do we play nice or do I throw the rule book out that window for as long as it takes?" he suggested and watched Mick sit back down. "That's better, so you were seeing this girl, dating her like Dunvega said?"

"Yeah, that's right, and...?"

"And, truth is, she was far more than just a neighbour and a passing fancy, wasn't she, Lannigan? It was serious then, at least that's how you figured it?"

"I make no bones about it, so what? *Hey*, wait just a frigging minute! Suddenly I don't care for the way this is going down, *again*! What are you *getting* at? Because if you're accusing me of having something to do with her death, you can *all* go straight to hell," he shouted, incensed by the implication.

"Whoa, tough guy; no one is accusing anybody of anything, just yet. Otherwise you'd have heard your rights already."

"Then ease up," said Mick defiantly. "You want co-operation, then level with me or else you'll hear my rights, and from my lawyer."

"I know, Nesbitt and Finch. Look, Lannigan, you make this easy—on me anyway—likely as not this turns into an afternoon social and you and I are old friends by the time I walk out that door. You want me to level, okay, I'll *level*. I think you know plenty. Your girlfriend gets blown up across the hall in broad daylight less than ten feet from your *goddamn*, from where I'm standing and you claim you don't know anything. Uh-uh, Mr. Detective, wrong! I have a stinking, queasy feeling in the pit of my stomach that there's more to it. It's either intuition or that frittata I ate earlier, or both," he admitted tending to the spot with a touch of his hand. "No, you're tied up in all of it somehow, and I also sense none of this is exactly virgin territory for you. Still—" The officer vacillated. "I'm willing to be gentle and give you even more rope if you like as long as you're willing to put out in return." He sniggered, looking over at the two officers, side by side and, all at once, causing him to wipe the smile from his face. "Rather than standing there like statues, why don't you get started," ordered the officer in terse tones, watching them leave the room and make their way down the hall towards the rear of the suite. "Be sure you do a thorough sweep. Don't overlook anything, including that john back there, this whole thing smells and something around here is definitely full of shit," he declared, suddenly looking back at the detective.

"Now, where were we? Oh yeah that's right, you were telling me to go straight to hell," he repeated, hauling out a small notepad from under his brown tweed jacket. "Suspect co-operative, nope, not so far," he remarked, writing something down and then lifting his head and staring in the direction of the sofa. The phone behind him rang. Leave it," he groused, looking around the apartment. "I'm sure even this place has an answering machine, am I right?" He grinned. "So when was the last time you saw...?" he began, interrupted by one of the other officers down the hall while the phone continued ringing.

"Lieutenant," he hollered. "I think you might want to have a look at this."

"I'll be back, Romeo. But while I'm gone, why don't you see if you can't come up with something I can use, and that's maybe gonna help both of us," grumbled the investigator. Clicking the end of his pen with a heavy thumb and shoving the ballpoint into his shirt pocket, Stern headed towards the voice coming from inside Lannigan's bedroom at the far end of the corridor.

After several minutes, he returned.

Mick was up pacing the floor near the window by the time the lieutenant came back. He was debating what kind of evidence they had on him to obtain a warrant to begin with and then suddenly, wondering what they'd found that could possibly connect him to Adella Hughes or her murder.

"Well, well, Mr. Lannigan, it seems like my men actually came up with something after all. What appears to be a letter in amongst some of your belongings, though to be perfectly honest, it's more tape than paper really, from the look of it. Written to, would anyone care to take a guess, a show of hands? That's right," he said, noting the agitation in Mick Lannigan's eyes. "'*Dear Adella.*' I think we have to conclude the dead woman, Adella Hughes? But it certainly begs the question, why is it still here or even more to the point, why is it here at all?" asked Stern, scanning the first page and eagerly flipping to the second. "Logic tells me she must've seen it, there's a lipstick smudge here. Again, I'll assume hers? It doesn't strike me as your shade and besides, your mouth is too big. So what happened? You decided to take it back before you blew off the girl and blew up the place with her and her new boyfriend inside? And being the clever detective you are, no doubt you deduced it would be somewhat incriminating if it were ever found in the rubble. Far more damaging than if it was discovered here, I guess?"

"I see," mumbled Lannigan, sounding perfectly calm and not the least bit disturbed or flustered by the most recent barrage of banter and aspersions. He was decidedly convinced the man was reaching for far more than he could hang onto. "It's that way is it? Well you certainly haven't let me down then. You really aren't very… *insightful* for someone whose job demands that he piece the clues together with some fancy footwork rather than making them up as he dances down another dead-end. What, you got a relative down in City Hall or are you sleeping with the Commissioner? Apparently, he favours balding men and from what I've heard, he looks pretty hot in drag, Sergeant."

"*Lieutenant*, Lannigan! It's Lieutenant," he barked, pointing a finger in the detective's direction. "And don't forget it, smart-ass! It wouldn't take much for me to take you down a few notches just before I take you down town to a holding cell on suspicion of murder for seventy-two hours. Maybe that would instil a sense of reality and respect in that twisted little …"

"Okay, I get it," he said. Considering his options and just like Stern, coming up short, the private eye realized he might've crossed a line and outdone himself this time. "Take it easy, I never killed anybody. I gave the letter to Adella, yes, for obvious reasons when and if you read it. But it wasn't anything like that fairy tale you just laid, Mother Goose. You'd think with all the practice you get, you'd be better at it and yet you never cease to disappoint me; playing hunches to the hilt, letting the chips, and the bodies fall helter-skelter, and then sweeping your mistakes under a carpet somewhere in a back room of the fifty-second Precinct." He hesitated, studying the man's furrowed face. "You know, maybe you jokers should listen more and think less, at least until you have *some* of the facts. I'm surprised you haven't learned you can discover a whole lot more by keeping your mouth shut instead of flapping your gums like some French, wind-up doll," he submitted.

"So talk, I'm listening. Lay it on me. Teach me, bright-boy! Prove to me you're an innocent bystander, I'm waiting. Tell me what it is I don't know."

"Look, I think you'll agree that neither one of us has that kind of time," he smiled, sensing the dynamic shifting. "But if you'd like, we can start with baby steps beginning with the truth and what really happened." He floundered, recalling the afternoon in question in vivid detail. "It was like this, Adella showed up pounding on my door. As soon as I let her in, she produced that letter you're holding from her jeans pocket.

After a healthy tongue-lashing—and not the kind you hope for—she proceeded to tear it up in my face… because of a silly misunderstanding. Anyway, I picked up the pieces, all the while pleading a rare form of intermittent lunacy caused by kissing beautiful women under the spell of a full moon and she and I spent that evening, amongst other things—" He digressed, recounting images of a proper tongue-lashing and snippets of an unforgettable dialogue before continuing his present one. "Putting it back together like some bizarre jigsaw puzzle and laughing about it," he confessed, looking suddenly solemn and somewhat troubled by the recollection. "Anyway, one thing led to another and, to make a long story a little more discreet, she must have left without it. I guess your trained hounds in there found it exactly wherever it ended up that evening," he added, witnessing the two men appear from down the hallway.

"The place is clean, Lieutenant. Drexler even checked the bathroom like you wanted. Except for a partially plugged crapper," he chuckled, "nothing-nada-zip-zero, a big goose-egg, chief." Mick grinned.

"No trace of anything suspicious other than that letter," reported Stokes. "And that's it." The lieutenant began poring over the document as Lannigan watched him.

"You don't need to read it, Stern. It means nothing to anybody…" he stumbled. "…except me now."

"That may very well be, but the warrant I'm holding says different. And something tells me your little affair ended badly. We've already established opportunity. I don't think motive is far behind," he said, averting his eyes from the paper to the detective and then immediately back to the letter in his hand.

Mick was tongue-tied, pained at hearing the notion, however twisted and surreal. He simply turned his back on all of it and walked over to the window. Looking down into the street, he was quickly reminded of his choice in women as well as the passion that caused him to forge the letter in the first place and, cursing the two-strike count, Lannigan admitted, to himself anyway, that he had no regrets and wouldn't change a thing.

'*Dear Adella,*

For what it's worth I accept you completely, even your version of common sense which is still under review. I accept your life, your love, your flaws—like mine, too numerous to admit to—your wit, humour, intelligence, charm, your refreshing unpredictability as well as your beauty, inside and out. I also accept that my fate seems to be to love you no matter what for as long as I'm able to sustain emotion. Most of all though, and more to the point, I accept what's best for you. All I've ever wanted from the first time I laid eyes on you was for you to be happy. Because of that, I'm willing to do whatever you need, within reason, to make it so. As much as it hurts, and it does—more than I care to confess—I respect, and accept, your decision if it brings you the happiness you're looking for.

I know you love me. I cherish the thought and appreciate how rare that gift is. More precious even than life itself, and as I've told you time and again, I'm grateful you decided to tell me. Now I feel somehow more fulfilled in the knowledge, permitting me to walk a little taller, appear a little stronger, try a little harder and dream a little bigger. So all I ask in return is that if you ever do stop, let it be your secret.

I adore you, and in ways you can't imagine quite possibly. I know I have from the moment we met. Every once in a while, you come across someone who takes your breath away, that was you. A kindred spirit from your first smile to the sobering scent of your skin and, what's more, I always will. That won't change, it can't. Love isn't a commodity that diminishes with circumstance, something that disappears or that can wither and die in the prevailing winds of time and chance and changing tides. If it did, it was never love to begin with, I suppose. Indelibly, you'll always be a part of what's important to me, and what makes me who and what I am, now and for as long as I live. Distance and absence can't deny that for me, nor will they ever. Maybe that's the difference between us, sweetheart?

Love isn't something you can just walk away from, not entirely even if you think it is the right thing to do. Still, whatever you want, I'll learn to live with, for you, 'as you wish', But the memories and the love we've shared, I keep...

*Yours forever,
Mick'*

Stern lowered the pages.

"Let's go fellers. We've done all the damage we can do here," he stated, staring at the back of Lannigan's head while the detective—half-embarrassed and the other half equally humiliated at the thought of someone other than Adella reading the confession—struggled with his circumstance, several apprehensions and roomful of critics. Then, hearing the man's, rumbling remarks, Brice Michael Lannigan quickly turned and faced the officer holding the pieces of paper. "Just don't skip town, Shakespeare," ordered Stern, casting a foreboding finger while Mick considered one of his own. "It wouldn't sit right with me, or the captain. And I can't speak for him you understand, but personally, I'm not done with you yet and, from the sounds of it, you aren't either," proclaimed the lieutenant tossing the letter down on the desk...

Part II

Chapter 5

I'm not a devout Christian by any means, but I read somewhere that Jesus died for our combined sins in what has to be regarded as a selfless act. If that's true, I'll certainly need to focus on mine more in order to make that wonderful gesture worthwhile— though after careful review, it seems my record falls sadly short of religious expectations, unless of course letting the church down is considered a sin in which case, according to the scriptures anyway, my soul is saved and all my troubles are over...

—WEDNESDAY, MAY 6th —7.00 a.m. —

"No! Just leave the blindfold on for the time being... till we're inside," ordered the gunman as the shadow withdrew his hands and instead, grabbing Mick Lannigan by the arm, helped their hostage from the back seat of the car.

Once the detective was on his feet, the same man removed the gag from Mick's mouth and untied him.

"Well that's a *little* better," he mumbled, massaging his wrists and spitting some lint off his tongue. "You know, it finally came to me over that last bump in the road where I'd seen you fellows. It was in the Mayflower, last night. The image is a bit fuzzy, but you're definitely the two pugs in pinstripes that ambled into the bar shortly before I left. You've been following me," he said, as if it was a revelation that had tugged at him for days. He stood next to the dark-coloured, late model Lincoln, still running as he stared into the underside of a pitch-black kerchief. But for how long and why he mused, being nudged forward by the barrel of a hefty gun at his back.

"He was right. You are a *cocky* son-of-a-bitch. But you're frigging loopy, you know it! Now just keep walking, Sherlock. This way," demanded the gunman, pausing and waving the stalk of his magnum as if Mick could see it. "Doesn't someone think *they're* the cat's ass? Are you sure that blonde didn't screw your brains out or something, Lannigan?" He laughed. "I don't know what the *hell* you're talking about."

"Sure you do! That's how you could find me this morning." He hesitated. "And the day before, I caught sight of two men hanging around across the street outside my building," he said. "You two have been tailing me for a while now, though it doesn't make a whole lot of sense. At first, I figured it was just my imagination; but, obviously I was mistaken," he declared as they led him inside an abandoned warehouse, a storage facility for Acme Truck Rentals according to the sign on the corner of the lot, and none of which the detective could see. Built in the early twenties, the property backed onto the Hudson River in the heart of the industrial district. Far removed from downtown Delray perhaps, but the metropolis of Conley was a mere stone's throw away if the chucker had a real good arm.

For several minutes, the detective wandered blind through the echoing halls, noting his steps and even counting them at times while snaking this way and that through the structure. With the hush all around, he could easily hear the wind howling across the river as he was ushered from one corridor to the next.

Then, stopping abruptly, all at once everything was still—even quiet enough to detect the palpitations in his chest ricocheting off the concrete walls. So silent, he listened helplessly to the shadow beside him breathing and, the man on his right, slide a finger from the trigger and slip the weapon into its holster beneath his jacket. Suddenly a door opened and Mick was made to go in. Before he could consider what was to come, an older man in a gruff voice, and with a discernible accent, ordered the two escorts to get rid of the bandanna wrapped around Lannigan's head.

The shadow wasted no time doing what he was told.

Once the man's sight was restored, there, facing him was a powerfully stoic-looking gentleman—well-dressed with a respectable amount of distinguished grey along his hairline and just the right number of furrowed wrinkles for a fifty-six-year-old underworld Mafioso.

God! Damn, thought Lannigan, not willing or wanting to believe his eyes. For a split second, he was nervously giddy, quite nearly appreciating the short-lived blindfold and then all of a sudden, spellbound, focusing on the infamous icon no more than twenty feet from where he stood. The man—larger than life with a reputation that reached back a generation and boasted more deaths than the Vietnamese War—was standing behind a desk in back of a sheet of plate glass, in a room that seemed endless it was so vast, and that verily mimicked his notoriety, cold, barren and boundless.

Along with a dozen or more ceiling fans buzzing overhead and spinning in unison, and as many portraits hanging on the walls, the location was completely void of windows. All of it presenting an ominous, and befitting, stage for what might turn out to be his own demise, he realized, easily based on circumstance and a conviction that was magnified by his suddenly, overzealous imagination. The only son of Irish immigrants whose father had been a cop till he disappeared one night and just never came home. The police conducted a feeble, inept investigation that, to Mick's way of thinking anyway, rivalled the progress made in the double-homicide that took place across the hall from him. And just like this one, there had been little to show for their clumsy efforts other than unsubstantiated hearsay, conjecture and a series of hunches based on the detective's last case. After several months, having never found any trace of his father's body, and even though the books never closed on the incident, the trail and the search for the missing police officer did. Seven years later from the day of his reported disappearance, Lieutenant Michael Joseph Lannigan was declared legally dead.

What could I have possibly done to piss off a man of his influence? How does he even know me from a stain on his shoe considered the private eye, spotting a pair of trap doors, one on either side of the desk? Did it have anything to do with the girl, he debated briefly, cringing at the thought she was somehow related to the warlord who, at that very moment, was staring back at him with an indignant and callous gaze? No, decided Lannigan. He didn't think so after recalling the conversation in his apartment with the posturing, hairy-knuckled, gun-toting goon no less than an hour before while he was attempting to get dressed.

Assessing his imminent future, apparently bleak at best wedged between two thugs, each capable of snapping his neck in a heartbeat, he immediately realized in the same instant that there was still a small flicker of hope. If he'd been kept in the dark as long as he had, it was likely he'd also see a return trip by the light of day, though under wraps no doubt if his reasoning proved correct.

On the other hand, he argued with himself, nothing in his life lately seemed the least bit logical. Not since that fatal day in March when Adella Hughes had been brutally murdered in her own apartment, he noted;

picturing her perfect features and lost in reflection, the detective was unexpectedly startled hearing a collection of gears and pulleys grate beneath his feet.

Momentarily distracted by the resonant rumblings, Mick stood apprehensive, though stalwart. His curiosity welled up with anticipation, combined with a surge of adrenaline coursing his veins and ripping at his weary soul. Now, he listened only to muddled notions in the incessant interlude with the lingering white noise and few clues to draw on. Eagerly waiting while the notorious celebrity studied his appearance from head to toe, yet again, and becoming increasingly anxious for the head of the Fandano Family to say something, anything…

Chapter 6

If it were up to me, I'd take my chances with the girl. She's much prettier in a dress and tends not to leave a trail of bloodshed. Well okay, she's prettier anyway…

Four miles away off the next interstate and inside the city of Conley, larger even than Delray, there was a man with enough answers to satisfy a number of curious trailblazers, including Mick Lannigan. Possibly Lieutenant Stern of the 52nd Precinct as well if he could get his nose out of the gutter and back onto the main highway and, yes, even G. Luciano Fandano once he finally got around to sharing what was really on his mind…

Chapter 7

If it's a case that you're after, a sobering refrain for your failing peace of mind come undone, then without further ado step this way, and welcome to the 'Wheelhouse of Misfortune' off Interstate eighty-one. The home of corruption and of cause and effect—that is, once you can suddenly see, clearly roping you into a philosophical fray, putting your well-knotted life on the line as they say, and at the end of a noose if need be...

—7.10 a.m.—

As the near invisible panel disappeared into the floorboards just in front of the detective's feet, and with little fanfare as it was happening midst the enormous, empty storehouse, the man behind it made his way around the desk.

Better known as the 'Sicilian head-hunter', the semi-retired, underworld icon lived as a legendary phantom might, a recluse deep in the shadow of seclusion somewhere at sea aboard his elusive yacht. Only heard of in private and whispered about discreetly behind closed doors, he rarely surfaced to receive outsiders, most especially bottom-dwellers and meaningless types like the one he'd suddenly summoned.

"So you're Lannigan," droned the worldly merchant prince, hobbling to his left and still flaunting a natural swagger from years of having to make the effort. "I'm not sure if I've been deceived or my expectations were too high," remarked Fandano, approaching the dishevelled private eye and stopping his advance within breathing distance of his guest's bewildered expression. "No doubt anxious," declared the dapper looking don, carrying the entire conversation for the moment. Showing a conservative smile several degrees below cool, but efficient nevertheless, all too familiar with the circumstance and keenly aware of the swirling dilemma daring Mick Lannigan's senses, he continued, "Wondering why these two fine gentlemen here, ousted you from your warm, cozy bed a short while ago? And perhaps why we've been thrown together in this unlikely scenario, you and I?" He paused. "And at such an ungodly hour," he added. "Like ships colliding in a south-sea squall out on open waters and what we could possibly have in common to talk about before it's too late," he declared in a commanding tone, throwing up an open hand, not wishing to hear any sort of response for the time being.

"Fair questions," noted Fandano, raising an arm and extending his index finger from a tightly closed hand. "All the right ones as a matter of fact," he chuckled briefly. "Still, I don't know how fair you'll find my answers, not that it makes much difference. 'That which does not kill us makes us stronger, in the end.' Soon you'll know the meaning of these words, just as I do, *every day*. And how close to the end you really are will inevitably depend on you, for this is a time of judgement *and* redemption. Circle it on your program, May sixth," he professed in crescent tones as a preacher would. He considered the stranger's intricate design, sizing up the recent arrival from head to toe in the fleeting silence and scrutinizing the detective's physique, mauling his unshaven chiseled chin with a sinewy hand and pivoting it effortlessly from side to side.

Mick never made a sound, but deep inside, his stomach winced and whined and, just like the outside world, turned on him unexpectedly. The frantic swarm of butterflies, suddenly panicking, wound their way and, flapping wildly, scraped the walls of the narrow, knotted route, weaving down and around through bowel and bile and then back again in search of an out as the onlooker only listened, squeamish, staring back at the man standing in his face. "In the meantime, your first answer is a simple one, and to my mind right up your alley having to do with, '*omicidio*', *murder*," he revealed. "*Vile, ruthless and cold-blooded*," Fandano rattled off then hesitated while his eyes swelled with a savage and sinister rage, mesmerizing the outlander. "My son's to be precise." He wavered but an instant, clenching his hand into a fist and then relaxing it as quickly. "I don't know who '*i maiali bastardo*'," he snarled, "the bastard is yet." His worn face was beginning to crease and resemble dried cowhide hung out in the Arizona sun for days on end. A possessed look of torment settled in as he gazed towards the rafters high above the whirling murmur of fans dangling from long, white conduit and cable. "I will though," he grumbled, "if it takes me the rest of my natural life, *and* yours, Lannigan. And when I do, *know this 'inglese'*, I'm going to string up the son-of-a-bitch by his balls, if he has any, and peel the flesh from his bones," he pledged, grinning quietly to himself. Contemplating as well—or perhaps instead, 'an eye-for-an-eye'—jamming a key of explosive in both ends of the unfeeling assassin, he laughed at the ridiculous whim, realizing it was far too quick and merciful. Then all at once, raising both hands, animating his intentions, he persisted with his wordy execution. "Next I'll tear every limb from his miserable body, one at a time and after I have his complete and undivided attention," he ranted and sneered, flip-flopping between tongues this way and that, mumbling his irreverence to the Lord Almighty. "Like I have yours now, I'll '*rip verso l'esterno il suo cuore*', and have it in my grasp," he insisted earnestly, entertaining the idea. He held up the palm of his hand and squeezed the limp, bloodied muscle as if it were there already, oozing the last trace of life from its mass. "His eyes spooned from their sockets and both lungs yanked from his asshole as he screams out his final, agonizing breath," submitted the old-world mob boss, finally taking one himself. "Then feed... *il figlio della a dogfaced la femmina*, piecemeal to the fishes in that river outside. All except his head." He paused, savouring the anticipation. "That I sever from his lifeless torso with my bare hands and burn till the skull is nothing but a scorched shell. Crush and *grind* the emptied husk into a pile of so much powder and dust in the wind, piss on the remains and leave the blend for the maggots to choke on."

"When?" asked Lannigan experiencing a time lag, at last able to gain an opening. He recalled a far-off rumour and was curious how long ago his son had been killed. Though troubled more so by Fandano's inspired, even obscene and perverse hostility and the reason for it, it was no less comforting as he grappled with his own whereabouts, and why.

"When, what?" barked the notorious head-hunter, still visualizing the time of reckoning and the concoction of pulverized bone and urine bubbling at his feet and cognizant, once all was said and done, that it still wouldn't be enough to secure the closure he both pursued and craved.

"I mean when was your son...?" mouthed the private eye, not willing to complete his thought, recreating his own hallucination and dark images of the murderer's grim fate. He tripped awkwardly over the man's obvious anguish while treating his hatred like a new friend and the vendetta, the punishment, as a personal aspiration before life dare return to some relevance and normalcy for the sorrow-stricken father.

"March tenth," he sniped, his tone terse and tedious, muttering the date into the detective's face.

"In Delray," Mick blurted out, recalling the very day and the details surrounding it, noticing beads of sweat over the man's forehead and dripping down one of his cheeks. The reveal matched his, he soon determined, mindfully wiping a trickle from his temple and becoming more convinced of the man's outrageous obsession with his absolute justice, pure and simple as the first answer had been.

"That's right, on Palladin Drive, down in Ledbury. Ringing any bells, Detective?"

"Some," replied Mick after a brief recollection, gathering his thoughts, most of them in a state of disarray. "The fellow in the apartment with Adella Hughes," he mumbled to himself, all at once grabbing hold of a flurry of explanations for his mounting concerns and in the same instant, writhing and wallowing in a handful of new ones. "In the explosion," suggested Lannigan, his tone spiralling to meet his body language.

"Yes," growled Fandano, "in the explosion!"

"Your son is, was, Frank D'Angelo," he whispered, presenting a suspicious tone. "But ..."

"But what... you dare challenge my veracity? You're calling me a liar!" Fandano exclaimed.

"No," conceded Lannigan, "of course not."

"Frank Giovanni D'Angelo." He faltered, picturing his son's face only days before the incident. "It was his mother's maiden name, and her idea. Intended to keep him out of harm's way ..." he acknowledged, "... and in retrospect, one more reason why I should've lopped her head off when I had the occasion to as well."

"And you mean to tell me that with all your resources and... and sway, you still don't know who's responsible?" Mick suggested, finding it difficult to accept. He half-heartedly glanced about the room for hidden cameras and hoped desperately it was just one more twisted, reality series from the FOX network. He was willing to embrace the notion that his dead bookie, Jack Runyan, employing some ultimate revenge scheme for finally beating him at his own game—kaachiiiing— had instigated the entire hoax from the very first moment he'd had an imposter call him, pretending to be his older brother.

"Enough, Lannigan," shouted Fandano and then immediately reduced the volume in his voice. "Yes, it's true. As absurd, *and* as humiliating as it all sounds even to these weary, old ears," he confessed, pointing to his own. "That's precisely what I'm telling you. And that's why you've been delivered to me now, *here*, how should I put it... to save your life," he announced, sweeping a handful of perspiration from his brow. "Interested, Detective?" But even before the private eye could respond, the silver-haired Sicilian continued with his homily. "You'll have to excuse me. I've not been myself lately. It might've seemed like that was a choice," he professed. "Well, it's not," he explained further, looking pensive and even more cold-blooded than the murderer he chased.

"But why me, I don't understand," said Mick, reviewing the man's dialogue and their candid exchange. "Why not the Galisano Brothers or Shayne Mason just up the river in Rockingham?" He deals in extremely missing persons, that is if you can find him, he mused, sniggering nervously. "Though I think he might've retired."

"You really don't get it, do you, Lannigan? I'd think it would be obvious by now," asserted Fandano, taking pause and wondering how capable the man really was.

Maybe I don't want to get it, the detective deliberated, balking and wishing he were asleep, or better yet, still in the arms of a particular blonde and somewhere else as he listened to the chatter of the man before him, dressed in black from the remaining flecks of pitch in his hair to the short, white gaiters covering his Dockmaster, wing-tipped shoes.

"Perhaps I need to spell it out for you? However, I have been led to believe you're astute, have a natural instinct about such things and are very good at what you do... on those rare occasions you're actually employed. But *I'm* certainly not convinced," he added. "And having had a connection with this girl who died so untimely along with my son, Adey something or other," he said, mispronouncing her name and all at once rudely interrupted.

"It's Adella! Adella Hughes, not Ad—" announced Lannigan, wavering, suddenly feeling his right arm being seized and held, and then squashed like a child's squeeze toy. Mick flinched feeling his knees buckle beneath him and still he never took his eyes off the man.

"Like I was about to say, you have an interest here as well. Possibly even greater than you know," he continued, ignoring the comment and laughing, conscious that his point had been made. "And finally, my Irish hawkshaw, according to police reports, besides being a potential witness in the investigation, you also seem to be a prime suspect in their books. That makes you, to say the least, a practical commodity for my purposes either way," he said, locking eyes with the wary visitor. "So, in light of your circumstance and the proposal made by one of my most trusted, here's what I'm gonna do for you, Mr. Detective. I'm gonna to give you a truly rare opportunity indeed; in fact, the chance of a lifetime, *yours* to be precise," offered the sea-faring Sicilian, grinning like the newest lottery winner as he reached into his jacket...

Chapter 8

If you should rise by a gun, beware your fall with the son; there's no free rides, free-for-alls or free pass. 'No one here's turning back,' said the man dressed in black, 'man, you're in it right up to your ass'…

—7:45 a.m.—

Why is he telling me this, thought Lannigan? Made nervous by the questions and what provoked them, he was bothered especially by the term 'prime suspect' that his host had made reference to. In a flash, the telltale notion was searing his psyche like a branding iron on flesh, finding tendon and bone and giving birth to more fears than a phobia convention, listening to the persistent whir of fans overhead. He's after more than just my services as a detective, Mick decided, revisiting the graphic imagery Fandano had gone to great lengths to conjure up, seeing the man finally remove his hand from a shirt pocket. Holding a fat, dark-leafed Havana that he made a point to admire, and brushing it gently beneath his flared nostrils, the Sicilian patiently, calmly and deliberately enjoyed the earthy aroma. There was more to it Lannigan suddenly recognized. Much more

and, as in life, nothing is ever simple *or* cut and dry—
his father reminded him—with the exception of
someone's neck on the chopping block.

"No more games," the detective insisted, sighting a
paradox. "What's your bottom line?" he inquired, half-
pleading, half-heartedly and aware he was somehow
teetering on the scales of a different kind of—what
some might judge as—justice.

"I like that, sliding through the bullshit and cutting
to the chase. Very well, my bottom line as you put it so
succinctly ..." he hesitated, placing the cigar in his
mouth and smiling insidiously while beginning to light
it, "... is your *ass*! And somewhat ironic since you make
your living by the seat of your pants, I'm told." Fandano
laughed. Then, taking a long, deep draw from the cigar
till the heater glowed blood red and exhaling a great
cloud of smoke into Lannigan's face, causing him to
sputter and cough, the Mafioso, judge and jury,
continued. "Let's call it a witch-hunt. You're a private
eye after all, so if you don't turn up anyone legitimate
given your *apparent* qualifications, your personal
feelings in the matter and the delightful incentive I'm
about to introduce, we'll know who, or don't I mean
which," he sniggered. "Is the depraved son-of-a-bitch I
want to get my hands on. For you see, by process of
elimination ..." suggested the man, grinning, grabbing
the ball of the detective's shoulder and squeezing his
point home, "... it'll be you of course," he whispered in
Mick's ear before leaning back and cackling like a

deranged madman. Then quite suddenly Fandano desisted, still staring at the Irishman firmly in hand at the end of his reach, knocking the ash from his cigar. "I'm sure the police won't mind another loose end tied up in a neat, little bow—though, they'll never actually see you again, if you recall that little diversion I made to your future earlier. They're happy, I'm happier and everybody walks away a little better off, other than you that is… *capiche*? So find the person who took my only son, and my immortality, from me, or no one will find so much as a hair on that Irish head of yours. Nor even your head for that matter, haha, haha… ha, haha, ha, hah! Hah, ha," he trumpeted, watching his slack jawed detainee reeling from the outburst.

Finding the grit and stones to deny his circumstance and doing an about-face, the detective gazed back in a brief moment of bravado. "You're aware they don't have one iota of physical evidence!"

"It's academic *what* they have, Lannigan," declared the Sicilian, finding the point tedious, trite and time taxing.

"Nothing, they have nothing," he went on. "Not a thing that ties me to either the explosion or their deaths, other than opportunity and maybe, a weak motive. But no link whatsoever to your son, I'm afraid," said Mick, tired of hearing all the disturbing accusations, though none of them any more disturbing than the one coming from the man facing him.

"And afraid you should be!" He hesitated. "Nothing except perhaps jealousy, bad judgment and the need to make a name on some level," claimed Fandano, visualizing his son and suddenly turning away in disgust.

"That's ludicrous! First of all, I had no idea he was *your* son... and whoever told you that is a *liar*," professed Lannigan, outraged. "I don't think you believe that any more that I do, or he does," he asserted, indicating the gunman to his right. "The allegations and trumped up, would-be charges are all figments of their twisted little game, looking for someone, *anyone*, to take the fall." He vacillated, seeing his newest accuser turn back around with the same intent and fervent fire in his eyes. Watching the detective scrounge his thoughts, his soul and his near-empty arsenal for a stronger, far more convincing barrage and, both men, certain he wasn't swaying anybody with his futile burst of blanks, were suddenly sweating bullets. "Sure, I lived across the hall," he acknowledged. "And *yes*, at one point I did have a relationship with Adella." Mick stumbled, clearly sensing Fandano's resentment towards her. "But then she called it quits, slamming on the brakes. Changing course one last time like the roller coaster ride it always was," he admitted, his volume plummeting to a near whisper. "I wish I could say I didn't care, but then I'd be a liar as well," added Lannigan, shaking his head. "To this day I still don't get it! I just don't understand her reason for wanting to leave Delray all of a sudden. It nags the *hell* out of me," he declared, thinking out loud while other thoughts drifted, searching for an overlooked clue. "But so what, none of that makes me a murderer! It would be like someone saying that because you have Italian blood, you must've known Mussolini for *God's sake*, equally as ridiculous."

"But I did know Mussolini, Lannigan, and quite well as a matter of fact."

"*Okay*, bad example, and not unexpected, were you witness to my brand of luck lately."

"Maybe you should just stop wasting your time, and mine. Face it, you're the closest thing I have to a sure thing. That's all there is to it, detective. And there's only one way I'll ever be persuaded you're innocent." He desisted. "Get me the real assassin, a living, breathing being and the proof to substantiate it so he can look into these eyes," proclaimed Fandano with forked fingers directed at his own. "So he can see my contempt for his pathetic and insignificant life, see himself succumb to the torment that would consume his every thought in his final hours and to experience the hatred and the wrath that will slowly, irrevocably, lash out like some freakish demon and end it in excruciating fashion."

Entranced by fear incarnate and seeing no way out, the detective conceded to the fate handed him. He had little choice but to play the cards he'd been dealt one more time. A new game, a new dealer and, as usual, they appeared from somewhere near the bottom of a marked deck someone else brought to the table.

"My usual fee is four hundred dollars a day if you're after my services as a detective, though I don't see that happening. But I will require expense money if you expect me to find anybody. The thing is you've threatened my life at a lousy *fucking* time. As it goes, I'm scraping the barrel these days. And as fortune would have me, I found it, my future staring up at me from the bottom of the keg. I'll need a car as well. Mine was stolen the other day."

"*Enough*," he bellowed, losing his poise quicker than he would regain it. "I hope you're better at finding answers than you are at listening. Are you completely *thick*? I don't care about money, cars or any of your petty concerns! I only want flesh and blood, and answers." He whispered, "Do you read me, Lannigan?" Fandano concluded as Snake threw a fist into the Irishman's mid-section. As he buckled, the gunman struck Lannigan with the grip of his .357, releasing a blow to the back of the detective's shoulders. He dropped to the floor like a bag of hammers, lying in a semi-fetal position, on the cold, unyielding concrete.

Slowly getting to his knees, he stopped, hearing the abridged version of the question again. "Do you read me?"

"Loud and clear," he groaned, straining to look up at Fandano. "Like a neon billboard… still, without some give on your part, you might as well just take me out to the river now, piss on it and save me all this grief hanging over my head. I'm a detective, not a magician."

Fandano smiled, finding room to contemplate the man's request and realizing that, if Lannigan was who he was after, he'd at least have the balls to hang him by. "All right, handle it, Paulie, and whatever else he needs, within reason."

"One more thing," said Lannigan, finally able to stand. "I figure I'm on shaky ground as it is, and in no position to be asking, however, I'd consider it a personal favour if someone could keep the police off my back for a while, particularly a lieutenant by the name of Stern."

Fandano took a long look before answering. "Done, is there anything else you've forgotten? Do you need a wedding catered or somebody whacked, detective? Maybe I should change your diaper, pat you on the head and send you back outside to play with the rest of the trash." He grimaced. "You're beginning to try my patience. Perhaps I *should* take your suggestion to heart and just rip out *yours*! Maybe you're going to be far more trouble than you're worth, what do you say, hawkshaw?" he demanded, holding his hands out at his sides, waiting for a response from the tall Irishman.

"No, you won't regret your decision. I'll get your answers for you, for both of us," he submitted, wondering where and how he might begin, all at once considering a tiny cove in New Zealand as an option, and a white, sandy beach near Christchurch.

"You're an unusual fellow, Lannigan, I'll give you that. Let's hope you're just as clever," he offered, studying the likeness of the man before him. "And somehow your cockiness and your swagger remind me of somebody I knew once, a police officer, a lieutenant, I think."

"Lieutenant Michael Lannigan," Mick replied as Fandano clenched the cigar between his teeth.

"*My, my*, what a small world, indeed," said Fandano, recalling his run-in with the uncommonly common man and taking an exceptionally long drag from his cigar. "Your *father…* is that a fact?"

"That's right, my father," said Mick sharing a strained look with his disgruntled host.

"I'm rarely wrong. I suppose that's part of what keeps me who, and where, I am. Mind like a steel trap …" he said, tapping his temple lightly while the rolled Havana pointed skyward. Lannigan watched the smoke from its tip being drawn like magic, like a fine silk weave towards the ceiling fan as the aroma of dark, Cuban broadleaf wafted above their heads. "…and a remarkable judge of character. He and I crossed paths only once to my knowledge a very long, long time ago. We were both even younger than you are now, I don't doubt," he added, seeming to recall the chance meeting. "Believe me, there aren't many people I take to… especially cops. But your old man, well, he was different somehow. He had moxie, your old man." He laughed. "Charisma, and balls as big as your fist, still, he never struck me as a cop." Fandano paused, taking a second to scrutinize Mick's face. "He was the cop that just vanished one day," he said, looking pensive.

"Yeah, he was, and I don't suppose *you'd* know anything about that?" inquired Lannigan, playing the shamus and willing to cross lines drawn in the sand.

"I'll do us both a favour, detective, and forget I even heard that," he snarled while a profound silence swallowed the room temporarily, as if choked by the exchange. Then, finally dislodging his sentiment, the air seemed to clear and Lannigan continued.

"So how did you know my father?"

"The good lieutenant stopped by one night on business, his, at a bar I was frequenting at the time, 'The Lady Slipper' as it was known then; however, like your old man, it's not around anymore either. I happened to be there and a few of my, over enthusiastic staff, shall we say, took it upon themselves to present him to me like some trophy when he started asking a lot of irritating questions."

"And?"

"And we discussed politics. I explained the boundaries of territory and violated expectations, mostly mine, and he listened... *respectfully*! He was a man's man, confident. Not arrogant though, I admire that. He was from the heart, all right." He said. "And then he left. I never saw him again. Funny how that few moments left such an impression on me for all these years. Must be that curse of a steel trap, I guess. And now it's your time, though, unlike the inquisitive lieutenant who came before you, I *will* see you again." He grinned.

"I don't suppose you had anything to do with a car accident the other night up near the racetrack, or an insurance company interested in my services?"

"You see," he stated, slapping the detective's chest. "One more reason why I considered Mr. Tagliano's suggestion and this arrangement the minute I heard it. You're quick, Lannigan! Just like your father was," he said with a foreboding smile. "But as the lieutenant obviously found out, there's a fine line between quick... and dead. I'm curious what side you'll end up on." He laughed. "But remember, my people will never be very far away, so don't get any cute ideas. Now get the *hell* out of here," he concluded, holding up his fingers in a backhanded display and forming a peace symbol of sorts. "Two *days,* detective, the rest of this one and tomorrow, that's how much confidence I have in you. So find me the *bastard* whose life I want, and the one man who'll extend yours," he demanded, turning around and walking away. "I'll be waiting, Mr. Lannigan," he said, his voice booming, echoing. "In consequence, I'm inclined to reserve judgment till then, but not a moment longer," he added, sitting down and watching the three men leave the same way they'd entered as the panel separating them began to re-emerge from the floor. "If not, you won't see the light of day on the next, so make us both proud," he declared, giving up a smile. "And speaking of your father, I also suspect this is one more time you might think about following in his footsteps. I suggest you think again. These men here will see to it you don't." He laughed briefly, rolling the cigar over in his fingers while a discriminating look replaced his guffaw. "So long, detective; and, Snake, be sure to take good care of our friend there, for now anyway." He grinned, showing a hint of overbite.

While Mick Lannigan was being blindfolded, Fandano checked his watch to see if it was eight o'clock, as the sound of an approaching helicopter arrived outside, right on schedule...

Part III

Chapter 9

By a single act of violence, two lives were ended senselessly. And if I can't find their killer, it seems the third might well be me. Yes, an apparent random act has breached every line drawn in the sand for the two shipwrecked survivors still at odds, beached on dry land...

—IN DELRAY – 8.50 a.m.—

Mick Lannigan was taken back to Ledbury, where he was dropped off outside of his apartment building.

"Here's two grand and a promise that I'll be in the neighbourhood, Sherlock," offered Snake—who inherited his moniker by a choice of weapon, a .357 Python, tucked away for the moment—handing the detective a small, sealed envelope. "I'll arrange for a car; it should be along about noon," he said while his partner held the sedan door open for the detective.

"Maybe you could trim some time off that ETA Sidewinder? Remember what the big man said, 'Be sure and take *good* care of him'. In other words, make this Sherlock happy. Keep in mind that when I do find his son's killer, I'll be Fandano's next best friend, if only

87

for a little while, though still long enough to have his ear," suggested Lannigan. "No thanks to some people I'd say, or couldn't have done it without him. It's up to you, Mr. Snake, but I got to be honest here, with less than forty-eight hours, well, I'm thinking I might be a whole lot happier," he grinned, "if I wasn't twiddling my thumbs and a substantial percentage of the rest of my life away, if you follow me, and I'm sure you will," declared Mick, sliding out and stepping from the vehicle up onto the sidewalk as the door behind him slammed shut. Turning back around to see the Lincoln speeding away, he yelled, "Hey! How do I get …" he lowered his volume to nearly a whisper, realizing the futility of his efforts, "… hold of your boss," he muttered, the last syllable almost inaudible even to him, while he watched the car drive off down Palladin.

Before the sedan could disappear out of sight, Lannigan had already entered the building. He raced through the lobby and then waited for an elevator, impatiently jabbing at the call button lit up just above an ashtray barely bolted to the wall.

After several minutes, it arrived. He got in alone.

"Morning, Mickey, it's only just nine, but I get the feeling you're already having a busy day," stated Doris as he strolled into the apartment, breathing heavier than usual. "I met your new playmate, Ms. Carlisle, back there. I can see why you're panting," remarked his secretary. "She's waiting for you, and my guess is exactly where you left her."

"Thanks, Doris, and aren't you in a feisty humour this morning," he replied, surprised to see his .45 lying on the side table and, all at once, able to make some logic out of the earlier commotion he'd heard while being escorted from his apartment. Without breaking stride, the detective snatched up the empty pistol, strutted down the hall past the inquisitive brunette and then disappeared into the bedroom with a sudden sense of urgency, watching the blonde leap off the mattress and into his arms.

"Oh, Mick, thank *God* you're all right," exclaimed Cassandra, noticing his weary face, darker even than the shadow of stubble beginning to consume it and wrapping her arms tightly around his neck. "Who were those fellows? And what was that all about?" she asked hugging him and nuzzling an ear.

"Two goons and a case of mistaken identity," he said, lifting her up and setting her aside out of the way like a store window mannequin. He hastily yanked a clean shirt off its hanger from the closet and heard several pings as the metal wire hit the floor and bounced about around his feet.

"Then they thought you were this other fellow?" she replied while he put his shirt on.

"Let's just say I met a man who has suddenly taken an interest in my life. Or what's left of it, whoever I am, and just leave it at that," he replied, grabbing his shoulder holster off the bureau, quickly strapping it on and sliding his ivory-handled silent partner into it.

"What's that mean?"

"It means I don't have much time at the moment to explain what that means," he stated, rooting through his dresser drawers like a nervous burglar. For a minute she didn't say anything, only watched him slam each one shut in turn. Finishing the routine empty-handed, he immediately broadened his search, gazing around the bedroom as she spoke up.

"Listen, baby, I didn't quite tell you everything last night."

"Trust me, Cassie, now isn't the best time to correct that oversight," he said, looking at her, experiencing a twinge of guilt and unable to see past her pouting, puppy-dog eyes. "Okay." He floundered, spotting a pair of rolled up 'black-diamonds' on the floor in a corner. "Make it quick though. I haven't got all day, gorgeous." He hesitated. "But that's about all I do have," he declared, eyeing the alarm clock and watching his time tick and talk itself away.

"I'm convinced he's trying to kill me, Mick. My husband, I mean, I think he wants me dead," she insisted, in his borrowed bathrobe, but looking like she'd just stepped out of a salon.

"*Murder*, you're saying he wants to kill you? No you're right, you didn't mention that little detail. Why? And what else aren't you telling me?" asked Lannigan, sitting on the edge of the bed next to the blonde, pulling one of his socks on, and then the other, suddenly distracted from his dilemma by what she was preparing to divulge.

"The thing is his previous wife died under well, mysterious circumstances shortly after their honeymoon he said, though only after I'd confronted him about it. He suggested it was natural causes and that she had some kind of brain aneurysm. At the time, I thought I was in love with him, Mick, so I was willing to believe just about anything he told me, I suppose. Anyway, I began asking questions about his first wife, who'd left for no apparent reason according to him, ending up somewhere around here as a matter of fact." She wavered, reaching for her handbag. "Then I found a life insurance policy he never told me anything about, that pays double for my accidental death if you read the fine print. And naming him as the beneficiary in letters, big and bold as you please! It started me thinking," she said, physically shaken by the admission and, dipping into her purse, removed a folded document. "Anyway, I got scared and that's when I decided I was leaving him for good. I wasn't staying to ask him about *anything* or listen to any more of his flimsy, cock-eyed stories."

Mick took it from her, got up and walked to the door. "Nothing personal, believe me, but I have to leave as well, gorgeous. Get dressed," he ordered while unfolding the paper to examine it.

"Where you goin', Mick?"

"It doesn't matter. Stay here, I'll be right back. Meanwhile, just put your clothes on," he told her, all at once drawn to the woman's extraordinary features, even more striking in the sunlight, streaming through the half-open blinds when the garment she wore fell open. He couldn't help but smile, admiring the blonde's shapely form, scantily clad in a Victoria Secret's pink bra and matching panties. Hypnotized by her graceful charms, he watched her shed the gown and reach for a pair of nylons hanging on the back of a chair as he left the room.

"Listen, Doris, something's come up," Mick began, glancing over the policy on Cassandra Carlisle's life. "In fact, a number of things, none of which you might consider predictable or run-of-the-mill," he admitted, gazing up while still hanging onto the parchment. "It looks like I'm in a tight spot here, even for me, if you can imagine that; somewhere between a rock, a bigger rock and this really fricken hard place with a river at the end of it, so I have a favour to ask you, brown-eyes."

"Brown-eyes, huh, when it starts like that, my guard goes up, Mickey. What is it this time, a check bounced and the bank called? The racetrack beat Dunvega to the finish line for the rent money? Or am I to be collateral for another loan, how much do you need?"

He grinned, realizing of course, that any other time, she'd be absolutely right. "Colourful character assassination, but you forgot gambling debt and getting my life out of hawk. I wish it were only that simple, *and* that easy, darlin'. Unfortunately, it doesn't have anything to do with money and, except for possibly fathering a child, it's the furthest thing from my mind. No, the truth is, Ms. Carlisle is in a bit more of a jam than I was first led to believe. Her husband, who she tells me she's left for good, wants to end their relationship as well, but somewhat more permanently in his version allowing him to collect on a life policy," he informed her. "It seems he's willing to *commit* all right, but has a serious problem with staying power."

"I see," she acknowledged, looking as though it came as no real surprise and giving the impression it even made sense to her on some level.

"Tell me, Doris, you're a pretty good judge of character and, to be perfectly *blunt*, I can't see the forest for the trees after being in the bush sometimes." He smiled, winking at her. "So how does she strike *you*?" he asked, detecting a stark coolness in her usual warm demeanor.

The brunette took a minute. First to consider her personal feelings for the man, then to reconcile his loose, over-indulgent lifestyle, tried and tested time and again, and finally attempt to make sense of his recent tryst with the woman holed up in the light and shadows of the back chamber.

Doris Harrington was well aware she had the power to influence the private eye and that he trusted her opinion implicitly in these situations. It was one of the reasons why he conducted many of his interviews, with questionable clients particularly, in her presence. Still, he also had an uncanny knack for knowing when she wasn't being completely truthful as well. Part of the attraction, she supposed, and her kindred connection with the Irishman almost from the day she started working for him.

"You know, I only spoke with her for a minute or so. You really can't tell much from a few minutes with someone."

"Come on, Doris, quit stalling. I've seen you size up a man with an incidental glance, a single phrase or just a hand gesture. You're even better with women, now spill. It's me for crying out loud."

"Well she's glitzy, Mick. Rodeo-Drive-a-la-mode like a fancy dessert for a start, and the girl wears too much lipstick, especially this early in the morning," she offered. "I *can* tell you that for a blonde, she's no dummy. She can wrap her tongue around more than a word or two. Ms. Carlisle in there knows just what to say to men and just when to say it too and, yet, I can't *not* like the girl." She hesitated, looking pensive.

"Well then what; what is it, Doris?"

"It's just that even without her admitting it, I got the sense she's worried about something and that she really is in a lot of trouble, Mick, or at least thinks she is anyway. There's a certain vulnerable quality in her voice. I don't know how to describe it, a lilt that betrays her confidence."

"A lilt?"

"Yeah, a dignified innocence, like a frightened child, that gives her away. As though she's preoccupied by some nagging apprehension that's out of her control, but that she won't submit to. That's about it. She's for real though, I'd stake my life on it, and she's telling you the truth, about this anyway."

"That's all I needed to hear, thanks. *And...* on that note, I think someone has earned herself a holiday. What do you say?"

"That'll be the day," replied his secretary, snickering. "So she's a legitimate case then?" asked Doris, familiar with his affinity for blondes and his on-and-off-track focus lately.

"Amongst other things, yes," he insisted. "I can't lie to you," he said, plopping himself down on the corner of her desk and laying on a smile. "Don't get me wrong, I do try," he confessed. "I just can't pull it off."

"So what's the favour?" asked his secretary.

"I need you to take Ms. Carlisle back to your place for a couple of days and keep an eye on her for me. I have a deadline, somewhat more pressing, I'm afraid, that's staring me in the face and unfortunately, I have to take care of it first or I'd entertain the young lady myself," he remarked, getting up. "I'm closing down the office till Friday *anyway*. That means a two-day vacation for you... *with pay*," he said watching her reaction, one of disbelief. "So, how 'bout it, brown-eyes?"

"It's difficult to believe. I'm lucky to get paid on the days I do show up." She grinned. However willing to do just about anything for the man, legal or otherwise—though not prepared to let him know it—she hesitated a moment or two before eventually agreeing.

"Great! Look, give me a couple of minutes with her to explain things and then you can both get going. I don't have a clue about this wacko husband of hers, so I'll feel a whole lot better when I know you're out of harm's way."

"You mean, once *she's* out of harm's way, don't you, Mick, and *what*, only a couple of minutes? I heard you were better than that, Mr. Lannigan," she huffed, becoming uncharacteristically snide, irritable and incensed with him.

"Doris, what's gotten into you all of a sudden? I really don't have time for this right now. Cassie," he hollered, studying his secretary, who was quickly folding her arms in front of her, looking away and unable to face him, reconsidering her outburst and embarrassed by the comments. "Are you ready?" he shouted.

A few seconds later, Cassandra Carlisle appeared, approaching the desk.

"I've arranged for you to stay with my secretary here, Miss Harrington, for a few days. I know you've only met briefly, but she's a terrific gal," he professed, glancing back at her, straining to look past their recent exchange. "I'd trust the woman with my life, and have on numerous occasions whether she knows it or not. You'll be as safe with her as a baby in its mother's arms. I'm going to be tied up with another matter I need to tend to."

"I guess, if you say so, Mick," she said in dreary tones and a despondent look, seeing no alternative. "But before we go, I have to make a call," she said.

"There's no time for that," he insisted.

"Then we'll have to make the time," she replied.

"Girl, you're killing me here," declared Mick, hearing sirens literally he thought, rumbling up Palladin Drive, interpreting it as a sign of things yet to find him, and likely soon.

"I came to Delray with a friend," she confessed. "He was the one who suggested I hire you," she told him as a short-lived whitewash painted itself across Lannigan's face between the dark whiskers. "And it's not what you think. We're just old friends and that's all. He's more like a brother; although, I get the feeling he believes there could be more to it sometimes, but there isn't. The fact of the matter is—" she was interrupted.

"He might wonder where you've gotten to suddenly," suggested the private eye, conveying her concern. "Come looking for you here, and wouldn't that be awkward?"

"Yeah it would, so if I can't call—"

"It's probably not a real good idea," said Mick, picking up exactly where she'd intended him to, though taking a wrong turn somewhere. "There's no telling where your husband is."

"Then could you let him know everything is okay, that I'm fine …" She hesitated, brushing his face with a look he recognized all too quickly. "And in good hands. Tell him I said he can go back home if he likes, and that maybe it's best."

"What's his name and where's he staying?"

"It's Bettman, Brian Bettman. He's a nice fellow, Mick. Just a real nice guy is all. Anyway, he'll be at the Plaza, room six twenty-seven. He hates big cities. Too much crime he says, and perhaps he's right."

"There's no *perhaps* about it, your friend, Mr. Bettman, is dead right, you can take my word for it. Okay, you grab your things, and you, Doris, you I need to talk to," he said, pointing towards her chair.

She sat down. At the same time, the blonde walked over to him and, thanking the man with a gentle reminder, went back to get her coat and purse.

As she disappeared down the hall, he leaned over the desk. "Look, Doris, just to be on the safe side, when you leave, take the lobby and head for the Mayflower down on the corner. You'll know by then if someone is trying to follow you or not. From there, get a cab to the Connet Building on Industrial next to the train station; it's busy this time of day, real busy, so cross the street and take another one straight back here. If you are being tailed, whoever it is won't have time to turn around in all the traffic. And if they do decide to go after you, it'll have to be on foot, which means you can get a good look at whoever it is. Are you with me so far?" he asked in a near whisper. Doris replied with a subtle motion of her head that included a discriminating stare he didn't quite recognize, leaving the unexpected expression to declare a lilt of its own. Offering a brief moment of reassurance, Mick smiled as he gently grabbed her arm and, then stroking it, withdrew his hand. "You know I wouldn't even ask if I didn't have every confidence in you," he admitted, watching her and waiting as she forced a smile. "That's better, now when you get to Palladin, have the cabby cut through the alley to Jessup and then get him to drop you off a couple of blocks up from your apartment. Take the back way in just to be sure. Then phone me here. After that, no more calls," said the detective. "Promise me?"

"Whatever you say, Mick," said his secretary, frazzled by the gravity in his voice, but also calmed by his faith in her.

"In or out, unless it's me, and only from this number, *got it*?"

"Yes, I think so."

"Good. You'll be fine. Here, take this," he added, handing her four, crisp-looking one hundred-dollar bills. "That should cover your little sightseeing excursion and Cassie's room and board awhile."

"Where did this come from?" she asked, debating whether or not they might be counterfeit.

"Don't ask. Just take Cassie and get the hell out of here and, *no*, they're real," he replied, familiar with her skeptical side. "Oh, and ah... just in case," he said, already looking ahead to the weekend, "if it should happen that," he stammered, quickly backtracking. "I mean, thanks cutie, for everything," he remarked as the blonde appeared, made up exactly as she had been the previous evening from the three-quarter length coat down to her black stiletto heels and enticing, come-hither fragrance, to the diamond-studded earrings and red lipstick smile she wore wrapped around his arm in a nice little package, strolling out of the Mayflower together ...

Chapter 10

Sometimes being alone with your thoughts is the last place you want to be. Especially when you come to the realization that you don't have any worth considering, and the other ones you do have, scare the bejesus out of you. Suddenly it's far lonelier than you could ever imagine, imagining far more than you care to, staring at a blank wall, empty-handed, with nowhere to turn. Counting seconds instead of clues, feeling as though your head just might explode and, with that timely burst of wishful thinking, saving someone else the trouble...

—9.22 a.m.—

Lannigan watched the two women leave the apartment. He saw Cassandra glance back at him one final time, peeking through the receding crack with a forlorn expression. Catching a glimpse of Mick's eyes, callous, clouded and cool, she wondered what would become of him, them, of her, and what was so compelling that her would-be, white knight couldn't deal with the dragon breathing down her back. The one he'd been hanging onto most of the night.

Doris knew. She sensed all too well how serious his predicament was, and without him having to say a word. Eyes never lie, she'd say. They exaggerate sometimes, but they never lie.

As the door closed, the thought that he might never see either of them again became glaringly apparent, flashing across Mick Lannigan's brain like a ticker-tape parade in slow motion. Like a funeral march with a handful of mourners and an empty casket slogging through the streets. Without a body, lungs or a head and not a hair on it, all burnt to rat-shit, dust and cinders, crushed beyond all belief for only the maggots to sift through. 'And all the King's men couldn't put the Irishman back together again', he rhymed off, repeating the words, mumbling them as they rumbled through on horseback. Yet, all the while, he was tormented most by the idea of leaving Doris behind and, of the two standing out by the elevator, feeling sorriest for her. The thought surprised even him. Maybe he wasn't as shallow as he pretended to be after all, or maybe he was and he was just losing his mind. Considering the possibility, the detective consciously, or unconsciously, pulled a book off the shelf beside him: *Mafia – History, Hype and the Land of Opportunity,* located between an original copy of *Casablanca* that he was most proud of and his autographed paperback of *The Mason Chronicles*. A unique keepsake, having met the pocketbook-private eye in Rockingham one night, but still less meaningful were a choice ever to be made. However, the one he held—a factual account of the 'Family' Tree—was as thick and as big as an elephant's rump, he mused. 'I meant what I said, and I said what I meant, a head-hunter faithful one-hundred percent.'

A little over twenty minutes had gone by since Mick returned to the office. But with his life on hold, debating how fast a Snake could slither based on the fodder he'd been fed, and the odds-on-favourite feeding him, the man on the hot-seat sat in Doris's chair, swivelling back and forth mulling over his circumstance. Gazing at the blank walls in the empty room and then changing his concentration, Lannigan casually started leafing through the hardcover he still had in his hands. He watched the pages flip by but paid little attention to the contents on them. Instead, as he recounted the explosion that had ignited his impasse, fusing that moment to his present one, it suddenly occurred to him how few leads he had. The word 'none' immediately blazoned itself to the blank, black and white chalk slate inside his head and he stopped counting. Below his disappointing revelation was the letter 'F' in bold red print, circled like a teacher's score on a test paper and the image of Miss Carol, his fourth-grade homeroom teacher, raced to greet him just as she had every morning at the classroom door that year. The first woman he'd ever been infatuated with, him and the entire male staff of Viscount Alexander Elementary, and he smiled quietly, pleased with his recollection. Then, erasing the slate with one of the many brushes he'd cleaned for the blonde so often and, shaking it all off, Mick Lannigan turned another page.

With no clues, only a handful of hunches he couldn't trust and a trail so cold and frozen over he'd need an ice pick to uncover any tracks, the man was stifled, staid and stumped. He didn't have Jack to go on. All bets were off he grimaced, thinking about Gingersnap in the fourth and what he wouldn't be collecting because Jack was dead, "supposedly," Mick muttered, giddy and sniggering nervously to himself. Frustrated, wondering whose funeral he might get to first, he digressed, rooting for more alternatives. But other than an old friend, a civilian who worked at the 52nd Precinct and a little hustler by the name of Tiny, he had nothing but time—and very little of that—he determined. Then, opening the volume near its beginning as the spine cracked and the bindings ached from its inaugural visit, he began reading.

'*The origins of the secret society known as the Mafia are believed to be as old as the ninth century. During that period, Arab forces occupied the island of Sicily. The original inhabitants were oppressed and needed places of refuge to escape to. The word "Mafia" means "refuge" in Arabic. When the Normans invaded Sicily in the eleventh century, the native tribes were once again oppressed and forced into labour camps on the large estates that their rulers created. And once again, the only way to escape this fate was to seek refuge in the hills of the island. During every subsequent invasion of Sicily, the refuges established—'*

The detective stopped abruptly and advanced his curiosity a few more pages.

Starting to ponder why he was even bothering with the pointless pastime, he stumbled onto the blood, guts and the very glory and grass roots of the formidable, and historical, cult. Tripping as well over the undeniable truth, he also conceded that his life was no longer his own any more. He'd been shanghaied with a well-defined expiration date and condemned to death with but a tiny loophole that was farther removed from his grasp than the black ones far out in space, rarely found either—until it was too late. His last breath belonged to the Family and the backbone of the Fandano Family keeping the vigil, their head-hunting spokesman, proclaiming: 'you have thirty-eight hours, twenty-nine minutes and a few odd seconds left to save your ass, detective. Otherwise it's mine,' the private eye mused, listening to the endless dirge echoing off the inner ramparts of his skull like a metronome between harangues and guffaws. Seeing G. Luciano Fandano check his pocket-watch and lamenting over his imminent fate, in his own defence, Lannigan started perusing the passage. If for no other reason, to divert his focus from the ghoulish onslaught, the morbid malaise of mental masturbation at the hand of his life-lord and the twisted tendrils dangling and swaying effortlessly from the branches of the Family tree, choking him like

a noose from the neck up as he hung helplessly by a
solitary promise made to him.

'Omerta: A code of silence.

♦   *A vow never to reveal any Mafia secrets or
members under the threat of torture or death.*
♦   *Total obedience to the boss.*
♦   *Assistance to any befriended Mafia faction,
no questions asked.*
♦   *Avenge any attack on members of the
Family, as an attack on one is an attack on all.*
♦   *Avoid any and all contact with the
authorities.'*

*'By the nineteenth century, the Mafia had grown
vast, and strong, and where it initially had been a small,
partisan organization, it had turned into a large,
criminally oriented society, ignoring all forms of
authority except their own. At this time, the most
common form of extortion was the practice of handing
out Black Hand notes which started in the 1700s. These
notes, handed to wealthy citizens, were polite requests
for an amount of money in return for protection. Of
course, the only people that these victims needed
protection from were the same criminals who handed
them the notes. If the victims did not comply with these
requests, they, and their family, could usually expect*

violence, kidnapping, bombings and murder to be used against them as convincing arguments—'

Fanning the pages of the weighty book to the last few, looking for some ultimate conclusion or a magic 'bullet' he could conjure up and draw on in the event his investigation turned up nothing, he noticed several names in a paragraph, but one in particular that he recognized instantly.

'—Jimmy Hoffa[9], former Teamsters union president, was probably the most famous corrupt union leader until he mysteriously disappeared in 1975. Some say, this was at the hand of a rival madman, a maverick by the name of G. Luciano Fandano—

*The Mafia in the '90s is an immensely vast organization that continues to grow in power. The Syndicate... remains firmly in control over the larger part of organized crime in the US, while other parts of the world have experienced a large increase in organized criminal activity as well. Most notable among these **new** 'syndicates' are the Colombian drug cartels, also rumoured to be linked to the notorious Don Fandano, that were started in the '70s—'*

'[9] See Page 692 for details surrounding—'

The footnote was no more comforting as he glazed over the assumptive theory of Hoffa's death, from his mysterious exit to a supposition that Lannigan personally had, reasoning out where the butchered, beheaded and burnt remains might be.

Mick had read enough, too much in fact. Details weren't necessary he debated, contemplating a warehouse on the Hudson River and a man who managed to keep the fish well fed. The maggots weren't hurting either he mused, reminding him he was in way over his head for as long as he could keep it.

All at once anxious, trapped and cognizant of the corner he was in, the detective slammed the book down on the desk with a resounding thud, losing his composure and, needing to do something, anything at all, grabbed for the phone.

Dialling the operator, he asked for the number of the Plaza. Shortly after that, the desk clerk of the day was putting him through to room 627.

Mick listened to it ring once, twice and a third time, but there was no answer. Growing more impatient with each hollow strike of the bell and surprised by the man's refusal to pick up, he let it ring as many as ten times, teasing his temper before finally giving up and slipping the receiver back onto its base. He couldn't help but play with explanations. After all, it's what he did. At the same time, he knew he'd have to make a trip to the hotel to inform Bettman in person. Why? Because he'd given his word and when you're an Irishman, a promise is a promise. It wasn't as timeless and 'carved in stone' as the Sicilian Omerta and their 'code of silence', he mused; still, according to his father, Lieutenant Michael

Lannigan, it had been the cornerstone of the Irish credo for as long as he could remember. And although as a boy, it was a wily switch, green and slender, freshly cut from a birch out back, as a grown man, it was the 'Curse of Killarney' that would befall any mother's son who dared defy it. And as we all know, it's not what's necessarily true, visibly obvious, or easily proven that matters, but what we believe that makes us who, and what, we are…

Chapter 11

Just another headache, every day, and what's a guy to do when there's no chance to walk away? I took a tumble, now I've started to fall; my head is spinning hard and my back is up against the wall. I'm here beside myself just staring at the floor and I can't even hear the knock, knock knocking at my door...

—9.37 a.m.—

Nervously tapping his fingers on the tabletop, staring at the phone and waiting for the call from his secretary, Lannigan weighed why there had been no answer at the hotel. Bettman must be there, he mused; he has to be, recalling Cassandra Carlisle's profile of the man. At the bar he debated, thinking it would certainly be a consideration for him, contemplating the bourbon holed up in the top drawer no more than four or five feet away as the crow flies. On the other hand—though somewhat of a weak argument at any time—it was still only nine thirty in the morning, but choosing to keep his head clear for the moment, he let it be. In the shower maybe, he continued, playing the game, pursuing logic and wanting a resolution to the episode only so he might put it to rest and move on, something definite that he could sink his teeth into much like a dog chasing down a bone he knew was buried about because he could smell a revealing, tell-tale odour. He should be done by now, Mick decided. Quickly reaching for the receiver once more, the detective dialled the number from a pad in front of him in amongst a sea of doodles that included a box with a stickman inside clawing at the perimeter and trying to get out. He listened to it ring a half dozen times while studying the inane patterns he'd drawn, subconsciously adding to them and pressing even harder. There was still no response and he hung up. He'd try again later after Doris called. After something had gone right in his life for a change, he thought, glancing down at his watch. They'd only been gone a few minutes.

"Too soon," he mumbled, getting a little antsy, wanting Snake to show up with a car for him sooner rather than later and every minute it was getting that much later he thought, listening to the seconds tick down like a cheap, homemade time bomb. 'Hickory-dickory dock,' he rambled. 'The mouse ran up the clock, *kaboom*,' and he suddenly visualized Adella's angelic face in the flames at first, and then her body, disfigured and charred beyond recognition when it was recovered. It was identified only by dental records along with a small, 10K gold wedding band that he'd given her—it having belonged to his mother—and in a bittersweet reflection, he was astounded that it was found on a chain around her neck. If only she'd told me why it was over, why she had to leave Delray, maybe none of this would've… maybe I could've, he desisted, rubbing the back of his neck and feeling the tension gaining on him like a raging fire of its own.

Uncomfortable reliving the precise moment, wondering what it had been like for her and what she was thinking at the time, Mick took out a pad of foolscap from one of the desk drawers and began jotting down a number of ideas nagging at him—random fragments of a riddle that left him assessing what he knew, but more to the point, what he knew he didn't.

Soon his scribbling became concise. Detailed notes and an itemized list with best guesses, gut hunches: headings, sub-headings, times, dates, names and places, until a confession of sorts began to emerge in the likelihood of his death and finally, a personal will for Doris's eyes only rounded out the detective's efforts. A chronological outline of what could very well be his 'last will and testament', he surmised. Suddenly he looked up, feeling the cold, hard smack of reality in the face. He noticed a bat he'd caught in the stands at SkyDome one afternoon at a Jay's game, avoiding certain catastrophe for himself and those nearby when it slipped from Green's hands just days before he was traded to the Dodgers for Mondesi. And then who later went to the fucking Yankees anyway, he concluded.

Well, it wasn't a hot sunny day in August and he wasn't playing for the home team in the big game. Nor was it the bottom of the ninth, one run down with two men out and the bases loaded, and he wasn't stepping up to the plate in the game of his life, but it sure as hell felt like it. Right down to the scorching heat raising the temperature of his blood and the thirty-four-ounce Louisville slugger he couldn't take his eyes off, standing upright in a corner near the fire escape. He was content that he was ready for the next intruder who tried to throw him an inside curve or a sleight-of-hand changeup, and steal more than just a base.

Satisfied? Without a doubt, but it was also a game of inches, thought Mick as he tore off the four hand-written sheets, folded them up, and then slipped the pages into a #10 envelope.

Turning it over, he printed on the outside in bold letters, 'NOT TO BE OPENED UNLESS I CAN'T' and underlined it, all at once hearing footsteps coming down the hall just outside his apartment. He left the letter where it was, went to the door to take a peek through the security hole and, sensing his gut tighten like sun-baked, dead flesh on a deserted stretch of highway, immediately drew his gun from its sheath. Seeing nothing, convinced he was only imagining things and realizing Snake would just buzz rather than come up, Lannigan holstered his piece, relieved it was just his mind playing tricks on him for a change—or again—and turned around to greet the phone ringing off the hook. Doris, he assumed by the feminine quality of the tone, sharp and demanding. But at the same instant, distracted by his sexist assessment of the caller, like a spectacular crack of thunder overhead, swift, booming and short-lived, the detective heard a tremendous thud striking the entrance as the wood in back of him buckled. Unable to react in time, turn or even move out of the way, the door to the apartment flew off its hinges and into his spine, crashing the flat of his back and driving him face first into the well-worn pile.

Before he knew what had even hit him, trying to reconcile why a steamroller would be on the second floor to begin with and feeling like his back had just been snapped, Mick Lannigan, in a split second, lay motionless, totally unconscious and, to those in the vicinity, dead-to-the-world. His face was tucked into the carpet next to the side of the desk and the door of apartment 222, completely intact, including hardware, lay over top of him.

Standing in the entranceway and grinning at his handiwork, holding a .38 in one hand and rubbing a small gold-hoop earring using his thumb and index finger with the other, was a large, clean-cut man with dark hair and moustache, and a scar highlighting his cheek. Aware there was someone beneath the debris by the black wingtips sticking out from the end of the doorframe, he surveyed the interior sluggishly, not the least bit concerned and scanning the detective's quarters from side to side like a heartless machine with only a single purpose in mind.

Entering, the intruder immediately stepped around the panel underfoot, and the body under that, admiring his well-shouldered efforts. He witnessed the back of a hand, a man's, by the look of it. Reaching down and lifting the limb, limp and lifeless, off the grey shag and feeling around awkwardly with his sinewy grasp, the swarthy gunman wasn't able to detect a pulse. Then, crouching and moving closer still, he raised the one-inch thick panel above the back of the body and peered under, confirming only that it was indeed a man.

Though he was there to find Lannigan, the prowler hadn't a clue what the detective looked like and began rifling his trousers.

"Well, this isn't turning out the way I'd intended," he grumbled, flipping the empty billfold shut and tossing it down next to the late detective. "That's a shame, Brice Michael Lannigan. Born, June seventh, sixty-one." He paused. "And died—not murdered—but acci-fuckin-dentally, May sixth, two-thousand-and-something and who cares, haha, haha! Still, you disappoint me, flatfoot," muttered the home-wrecker. "Your head wasn't near as hard as I'd heard. Between you and me and this door here," he smiled, noticing a trail of blood dripping from Lannigan's ear, "I had a few choice words I wanted to let you have along with a bullet or two I was saving for just this occasion. But apparently my work here is done," he realized, getting to his feet. "Bang, you're dead," droned the burly gunman, laughing and pointing his weapon towards where he determined the detective's head should be underneath the battered board lying next to his feet. Firing several rounds into the hardwood, he watched the plank splinter, leaving two holes as the slugs burrowed into the yielding timber like a pair of groundhogs in soft soil and shifting sands, quickly swallowed up by the undeniable laws of physics. "But it's too late, you *son-of-a-bitch*, you're dead already," he griped, spotting an envelope on the desk; craning his neck to see what was written on it, he stepped clumsily, slip-sliding onto and then over the combination of obstacles sprawled beneath him on the floor.

"Hmmm, 'NOT TO BE OPENED UNLESS I CAN'T'," the man read aloud leaning across the desktop and noticing it wasn't even sealed yet. "Almost clever, eye-spy, but I think you fell short and a little *flat* in your attempt. Putting the cart before the horse, jackass, and sealed your own fate instead, haha haha! A piece of advice, flathead: 'be careful what you wish for'," he declared with a cockish sneer, cutting the air with a great guffaw that rumbled out the door and through the halls of the second floor.

"So can you, Lannigan… open it I mean?" He laughed some more. "What? I can't hearrrr you. Was that a 'no, I think I'm dead'?" The gunman grinned. "Okay, I'll take a look then. That's all right, don't get up on my account," he said, waving his hand at the piece of lumber, laying the gun down on the desk and picking up the packet…

Chapter 12

We all get fifteen minutes or a season in the sun. But time can wait for no man and when your number's up, you're done. So get off your ass and shake things up till the fat girl sings her song. Everything happens for a reason, Mick—along that narrow timeline— between dark and light, and right and wrong...

—9.53 a.m.—

Removing the collection of loose sheets, the prowler began fumbling with the pages, dropping several on the floor and watching them flutter under the desk. Anxious and beginning with the second page, the reader soon discovered that G. Luciano Fandano had hired Lannigan in a perverted sort of arrangement. "The head-hunter," he murmured feeling a profound ache deep in his groin. The name by itself sent chills through his body. As he read on, the chills quickly turned to screaming shards of ice crystals, sharp as razor blades—scraping nerve endings along the way and taking up residence in the base of his skull when it was revealed that the man killed, along with Adella Hughes, was none other than Fandano's son.

His mood changed, altering dramatically and swinging like a pendulum to meet his darkest hour. All at once, he felt frightened to death at the thought of what fate might await him as his heart raced faster and his chest pounded loud enough to wake even the dead. Snatching the fallen pieces from the carpet, he wasted no time ramming all four of the pages, as well as the envelope, inside his jacket. He was, at the same time, completely unaware that he'd dislodged a ring from his pocket, totally oblivious as it bounced at his feet, rolled and came to rest alongside the body of his latest victim. All of a sudden, he recognized that if the detective put it all down on paper, he most likely hadn't told anyone. Not yet anyway, and the man on the floor, with some of the answers, was dead he mused, undergoing a cautious sense of relief in the clarity of the moment, pleased by the knowledge that no one else would ever see the incriminating version Lannigan had penned.

Planning to destroy the document once he'd read the full contents, the intruder left the same way he'd entered, with far less fanfare at first, but certainly with a much greater urgency.

Then, stopping at the doorway and giving in to a second thought tugging at him, the dark-haired burglar unloaded his last bullet into the rug just beyond the top of the doorframe, hearing the .38 click empty. Missing its anticipated target, the round ricocheted off the concrete beneath, striking the window in front of the fire escape and shattering one of the panes in a cascading waterfall of broken and tinkling glass.

Running down the hall towards the elevator, the interloper experienced a delayed burst of adrenaline strike his brain while the reality of the letter penetrated deeper and deeper still into his psyche, generating a surreal flashback that saw only Adella Hughes killed and D'Angelo, the man who should've never been there in the first place, walk away.

***

Hearing the final gunshot on some level and stimulated by what was taking place all around him, Mick Lannigan became delirious in his personal purgatory and began hallucinating as he lay on his apartment floor.

"What the hell was that?" asked Lieutenant Lannigan of the 52nd Precinct.

"From here, it sounded like a gunshot," replied Mick, hearing the rattle of a window raining down, while behind him, he listened to footsteps fading in the fog between consciousness and light of day. "Whoever it was, they just left. *Jesus*, it's like Grand Central Station around here all of a sudden."

"I think you're right, kid. I don't hear anything anymore."

"Things like this have been happening to me for about a week now. I can't explain it, but it's just one thing after another," admitted the younger Lannigan.

"That may well be, but don't forget what I taught you, kid; everything happens for a reason. I've beat that into you since you were old enough to take a whoopin' like a man, and it was usually for a damn good reason." He laughed. "You've survived everything else up to now, what makes this time so different?"

"The fact that the man they call the Sicilian Head-hunter wants to slice and dice my life away if I can't accommodate him and find someone in the next—" he looked, but couldn't see his watch, "day or so. Dismantle me like a prime heifer to hear him tell it, and I *have*. Then set my severed head on fire, nosh the husk to the maggots and whatever's left, he'll feed to the fish just like he did Hoffa," Mick claimed. "And believe me, all I've got to go on guarantees me that free ride to the bottom of the Hudson," he said, taking pause. "I scratched out a string of possibilities before *this* happened, but none of them take me anywhere!"

"Now before I go any further, kid, let's just get one thing straight. Keep in mind here you're putting all these words in my mouth, so be careful what I say," he insisted, baring his teeth, Mick picturing the lieutenant smiling at him like he'd done when he was the kid his father referred to. "But that's just a load of crap," declared his father. Hogwash! Take a breath. Nothing's ever *that* bleak, think about it. Take your best hunch for crying out loud. There are *always* clues if you know where to look. It's been my experience that whatever you're searching for is, very often, right under your friggin' nose. Like with that blonde you tumbled onto if you'll excuse the pun, ha. There was a stroke of luck. *Like you with her*, not really sure about her story. You couldn't see the forest for the trees, you said. Horse-cackle! You just couldn't see it because you were concentrating on other things like saving your ass and a few lousy body parts. That's your incentive, son, but it shouldn't be your focus."

"I know, Lieutenant, but Adella never had any enemies. Still, she did want to leave suddenly even though she planned to put it off until the end of the month. And that's another thing that continues to haunt me, *why*? It wasn't because of me, surely? I can be unruly sometimes, *hell*, I learned that from you. But she and I were good together when it was good. And when it was, it was off the scale." He faltered an instant, recalling one particular moment. "She *was* married for a bit, but even that was a while ago—her husband *maybe*," he said, and though unaware of its origin, all at once Mick heard the doors to the elevator slam shut, taking his intended murderer to a car waiting outside.

"That sounds promising. Who is he, this husband? What's his name?"

"I don't know. She never told me. She didn't talk about him, or their marriage. It was as though they didn't exist, or she didn't want them to. Whenever I'd bring it up, she'd avoid the issue altogether, change the subject or leave the room. Do you smell aftershave, Aqua-Velva, I think?"

"No, but then I'm only a figment of your imagination. Maybe it was some kind of denial? Check the hall of records down at City Hall."

"Like I said, I don't have a name!"

"You don't need one. Didn't I teach you anything?"

"I'm beginning to wonder." He hesitated. "Anyway, they were married out of state and that's about all I *do* know. I couldn't even tell you if they were legally divorced or not," he confessed, having assumed all along they had been.

"Then call, or go there if you have to," he suggested.

"*Where*, besides, I don't have the time, Dad! Look at me, out cold and face down with a mouthful of shag on cheap, threadbare carpeting that smells an awful lot like the floor of a taxicab. I'm staring at a life span shorter than a fruit fly, most likely in a neighbourhood that won't find me unless I haul my own sorry ass up and walk out of that door there that's lying on top of me. Come on, you were a lieutenant for almost fifteen years, and a damn good one. Help me out here, what do *you* suggest?"

"I suggest you go with your gut, your raw instinct, that's what you're good at, kid. And I still believe everything happens for a reason. Deep down, so do you. *Use that*," said his father's voice, detecting the end of his visit and their short-lived reunion. "It looks like I have to go. I think you're starting to come around. That was the buzzer and I think you have company. Oh, and don't bother asking why I never came home all those years ago, its ancient history. Part of your problem, and what's more," he smiled, "it would only be your best guess anyway, right? So leave it at that and get on with your life, Mickey. Just remember, something will turn up, I guarantee it. It always does and usually when you least expect it, kid."

"Well I hope it's soon, Lieutenant," he said to himself, feeling groggy on a scale from one to ten and unable to make out the numbers. Fading in and out somewhere between dark and darker, but was able to hear the faintest rumblings of an intercom buzzing way off in the distance just above his head and on the other side of the door…

Part IV

Chapter 13

"Hah! Head's up, Mr. Sherlock," said the reptile with a grin. "You knew darned well I was a snake and either way, I'm gonna win. So get back on your high horse and appease the man in black; otherwise, they'll hear your cries from here to hell and back," ssssssssighed the Snake...

—10.02 a.m.—

Snake buzzed Lannigan's apartment again, but there was no response. He leaned on the button for several seconds and then let up, willing to wait a time or two. Then, stepping back, the man heard, and turned to watch, a car squealing away down Palladin like the driver inside might be late for his own funeral, he surmised. When there was still no answer, Snake decided he'd go up, entering the empty lobby. Making his way to the second floor, he discovered the detective, still unconscious, near the entranceway.

Bending down, seeing some blood on the side of his head and eventually locating a pulse under Lannigan's jaw, the visitor started smacking the private eye's face repeatedly with the back of his massive, sinewy hand and more enthusiasm than was really necessary. After only a handful of blows, he finally witnessed the man slowly open his eyes.

"Whoa, hey," exclaimed the downed detective grabbing his wrist.

"You hit me any harder," he said, not yet aware of exactly who it was doing all the slapping—and bringing a bit of a riled up spirit back with him from his stint in the netherworld of coma-central—"likely as not, you'll put me out for good." He declared, letting go and glad to be alive, though leery at the thought of who it might be. "If you're trying to help, then ease up on the patty-cakes; otherwise, just get it over with," he suggested. "I don't think it would take much. And if you're trying to slap me senseless, you're too late, I'm there," Mick admitted, dizzy and out of sorts like there was a helicopter blade whirling out of control inside his head.

Snake backed off.

"Good you've rejoined the living, so what the hell is this all about?" he inquired, kneeling next to him.

"*Snake*," said Mick, somewhat relieved, attempting to push himself off the floor with the flat of his hands, but quickly feeling a weight on his shoulders and his back to a wall in the form of a hefty door balancing on it.

"Yeah, your car's out front," replied the swarthy Italian, lifting the wooden plank off Mick's back and, in the same movement, leaning it against the desk, watching the detective struggle to gather his footing. "So what happened?"

"Someone muscled their way in and rear-ended me, owww," Mick winced, stopping a moment till the pain making its rounds let up and moved on. "*Shit* that smarts," he exclaimed, wiping some blood from his cheek, tracing the source to his ear and looking concerned by the disclosure.

"You'll live," replied Snake, studying the reaction on the man's face. "And you had better for your sake." He laughed. Mick said nothing, pondering who his assailant could've been and what he was after. "I guess you can be grateful these slugs didn't find their mark," stated the bodyguard, examining the pair of scars in the marred piece of hardwood. "One of these inside doors here and well, all your worries would be over. *Man*, whoever it was sure did a job on *this* place. *Someone* definitely wants you dead, Sherlock," Snake asserted, looking at the broken pane of glass under the window overlooking the back of the building.

"Well, the bastard will just have to take a number like everybody else," he said, still trying to get his bearings. Massaging the back of his neck and attempting to recall a lucid conversation from while he was out, Lannigan discovered a ring lying on the floor beside him. He quickly picked it out of the pile.

Familiar with the owner, Mick put it in his pocket thinking that Cassandra, not wearing hers, had dropped it from her purse sometime the night before. "You didn't by any chance happen to see anyone leaving the building when you arrived?"

"Yeah, as a matter of fact, some pug in a grey pinstripe with a moustache and some kind of candy-ass jewellery in his ear. He jumped into a car and drove off like a bat out of hell. Was that him?"

"I don't know. It could be," Mick confessed, feeling woozy whenever he moved suddenly.

"So what are you telling me, that you didn't see who did this to you? Any of it?" enquired Snake while looking around at the remodelling scheme.

"That's *exactly* what I'm telling you."

"Some fucking detective you are!"

"Whoever it was, busted that door down—" he pointed to the opening and then adjusted his aim, "—and the next thing I know, I'm eating shag for breakfast almost alone, in the dark, and counting enough stars to be declared my own galaxy," he replied, all at once considering the hour; glancing down at his watch and able to see it this time, though still not clearly. Clutching the back of his head, tender to the touch and quietly moaning his discomfort, he realized he'd only been out for a few minutes. "What kind of car was it, did you even notice?" asked Mick in terse tones, his pitch influenced by waves of pain splashing about inside his head. Adjusting his position, he sat on the carpet staring up at the man.

"Yeah, I noticed and it's more than I can say about some. It was a Grand Prix, fire engine red, and before you—"

"A Grand Prix, and a rental I'll bet," groaned Lannigan, paring the man off before he could finish. A small compact of course, he suspected, contemplating recent events and thrashing around the notion that if everything did happen for a reason, what was it? Then, suddenly, it dawned on him that he could've, should've, been killed, given the evidence. A game of inches indeed, but there were still only two strikes staring back at him, along with his personal valet and, deep into the count, tightening his grip, the batter stepped back into the box.

"Don't you *ever* interrupt me again, Sherlock or I'll finish what this fellow started. You hear me, *hotshot*?" Snake droned, glaring at the detective. "Now like I was about to say, I caught a piece of this guy's plate before he drove off, like maybe he was on his way to a fire, or to put one out. Anyway, I managed to get the letters 'XD' before I was distracted by this woman coming up behind me. And you can bet *her* sweet ass she won't be doing that again anytime soon." He grinned, visualizing how the paranoid intruder had run back down the steps screaming, with her handbag flapping in the air, breaking a heel and finally losing a shoe as she wobbled and flopped down the sidewalk while onlookers stopped in their tracks just long enough to scratch their heads.

"It's not much to go on, still, with your description, it might be enough. And speaking of advice, you really should work on your bedside manner," offered Lannigan, trying to stand, staggering a little and hanging onto the desk while he pulled himself to his feet. "If you're not pointing a gun at my groin, you're slapping me silly. Here's a thought, see if you can't find some other deserving schlep to occupy your need to make house-calls," suggested the detective, noticing the light on the phone flashing.

"Seems like a pretty big, fuckin' coincidence, this happening now, don't you think?" proposed Snake, ignoring the detective's comments altogether.

"I don't believe in coincidence, Snake, uh-uh, that's not how it works. I don't know what it is, but it's no coincidence," he replied, slowly coming to his senses and beginning to remember as he made his way around the desk. "The letter," he mumbled, checking the desktop, seeing only the book and recalling what he'd been doing before he was blindsided.

Mick checked all around the floor of the apartment, thinking the envelope might have been blown off with the motion of the door being jettisoned from its supports and smashing into his back. He looked for several minutes, but it wasn't anywhere to be found.

"Besides most of your mind, what did you lose now?" asked Snake, sitting back, watching intently and not sure what to make of the man any more. "Perhaps your bell got rung a little too hard after all, huh, Lannigan?"

"No, my head's fine. It's my sanity you need to worry about," he said, wondering where the pouch could possibly be and why someone, anyone, would bother taking the sanctimonious script of a scribbling madman. It was of no use to anybody, including him he contemplated, considering its content and most of his clouded ramblings. Then all at once his head began to clear, suddenly climbing out of the woodwork much like he had.

There *were* no other cases. It certainly wasn't a common burglary given the style of entrance. And nothing had been stolen that he could tell except for a collection of hunches, but perhaps one of them had struck a nerve. One of them must've threatened the intruder. That was the only thing that made any sense.

Very timely, he debated, thinking about Adella's husband and D'Angelo's killer, along with Cassandra's fire-breathing dragon who was breathing down her neck.

Then remembering her acquaintance, Bettman, on hold at the Plaza Hotel, Lannigan rapidly calculated the problems that were piling up like hot cakes on a hot plate at a Sunday morning fundraiser with no takers.

Grabbing his hat and coat, he checked the answering machine on his way out. There was only the one message and as he'd predicted, it was from his secretary.

"Mick, it's Doris, we're here and I thought you were going to be there. That was the deal, so pick up," she said in her throaty voice while he detected a slight lilt in her tone. "Pick up, Mick, I know you're there, quit clowning around, you big lug. All right, maybe you stepped out for a minute or something. Anyway, just so you know, we weren't followed. Maybe I'm a bit skittish, but there was a suspicious looking character watching us as we downed a cab near the Mayflower. Cassandra said he seemed familiar somehow. That's it I guess, although I was really hoping to hear your voice for a little reassurance. You were sure acting strange this morning. Stranger than usual, even for you," suggested the brown-eyed brunette as he imagined the perfect smile on her face. "I'm almost tempted to give that magician friend of yours a call to find out what's going on. I don't mind saying, I'm a little worried. I'll wait for your call, take care, Mickey. Bye for now," she whispered, hanging up. Lannigan did the same and the two men left the apartment together.

"What about the door?" asked Snake.

"What about it, it's broken and full of holes. You want to fix it, be my guest. Knock yourself out; then we'd be even," he chuckled. "But right now, I'm more concerned with fixing my life which, granted, is also full of holes. And if I can't do that, looters, landlords and living here won't be an issue, now will it?" he said, turning the corner. Moments later, the two men were down the hall and stepping into the elevator occupied by a much older man with a cane and thick sun glasses.

Once downstairs and descending the steps of 2261 Palladin to the street level, the detective saw that the vehicle Snake delivered was a '95, silver Intrepid. His own car and the one that had been stolen less than twenty-four hours earlier.

"How?" asked Mick. "Where did you find it?" he said, hardly able to believe his eyes. "I thought it would be scrap metal by now."

"I know some people, Sherlock. You're not the only hotshot with connections. I made a call." He grinned. "In fact, we would've been here sooner, but it took them a while to put the wheels back on and get all that fucking shit you had back in the trunk."

Lannigan smiled, impressed by the man's unexpected ingenuity and finesse.

"Just try and stay alive long enough for Mr. Fandano to get *his* hands on you, Lannigan, or he'll never forgive me," admitted Snake. "Oh yeah, you'll need these," said the sturdy Italian valet, tossing the owner his keys.

"No one's killing anybody, especially not me. Besides," said Mick walking up to the vehicle. "If you're so sure about me falling flat on my face again—" he paused, "—and won't find his kid's murderer, why are you going out of your way to be so cooperative? What's it to you? Are you hedging a bet or something?" inquired the detective, getting in and starting the car,

135

hearing the engine turn over, roar and wind like a saucy, little minx. First-time every-time he mused, listening to it purr like a spoiled tomcat and wondering if he was prepared to trust the man standing on the curb looking down at him through the open window.

"You might say that. I can be gruff around the edges, short-tempered and a little—no a lot—trigger-happy and have been known to have the occasional killing spree, who doesn't, haha; but that doesn't mean I'm shy a few bullets either, Sherlock," he said. "Now, *you* on the other hand, well, after finding you like I did and not even seeing who it was that nearly blew your brains out, a detective no less, I'm not so sure any more," he admitted, waving at his driver on the far side of the street to come and get him. "But if I *were* you, I might take a minute and check my gun," he insinuated, grinning from ear to ear as he watched the detective pull away...

Chapter 14

There comes a time in each man's life, when push resorts to shove. Where fate will turn the other cheek and just not care enough; it's why players play, the losers lose and the winners walk away, and how the innocence of all things good, like bullets, tend to stray...

—10.36 a.m.—

Lannigan arrived at the Plaza and parked in the hotel lot. The sun was bright, but outside it was still cool; he noted a crisp breeze blowing across his flesh as he stepped from the car. Tugging the belt of his London Fog a little tighter, he considered what Cassandra's friend, Bettman, would be like. Debating if he'd be in his suite and wanting to save some valuable time, he was determined to make it a one-stop affair. If he wasn't there, the detective would leave a cold, hard message with reception and that would be the end of it.

Time was at a premium. Mick hadn't even started dealing with his own muck yet, drowning in a quagmire of sarcasm, slurs and sludge up to his bloodshot eyeballs. He was defying death by dancing with a demon for a day or so and the most he had to go on was a hunch he couldn't pin down buried in a letter he didn't have and the man he never saw who took it. What he did have though was a full dance card, an endless string of bad luck he couldn't seem to snap and a possible concussion. Spoiled goods he considered, thinking about Fandano's plans, approaching the entrance to the hotel and wishing it were a pharmacy or a liquor store—or maybe both.

After negotiating a set of revolving doors, the private investigator crossed the busy lobby and, along with a crowd of others, piled into one of a wall of elevators waiting on the far side of the room. Like everyone else, he began jostling and being jostled inside the cramped quarters while beads of sweat trickled down his cheeks. On his way to the sixth floor, he was already pondering his next appointment on 17th Street, staring out at the scene below, hypnotized by the ever-swelling panorama coming into view through the tinted glass tower extending forty-five levels into a cloudless sky.

Arriving at Bettman's room, only a short distance down the hall from where he was let off, Mick knocked and, double-checking the number on the door, noticed it was ajar from the mere force of his rap. "Mr. Bettman," he said in a dubious tone, listing forward to peer in and sensing that something wasn't quite right. Discreetly nudging the door to 627 open the rest of the way, he could see drapes, mostly drawn at the end of the corridor, but little of much else at first glance in the poorly lit suite. Beginning to experience a queasy feeling in the pit of his stomach, the detective wasn't sure whether it was a subtle reminder, a gut hunch or something to do with the trumpets blaring while the siege on Jericho played out inside the walls of his skull.

"Mr. Bettman," he repeated, examining the bathroom off to his right at the same time. It was empty. The shower curtain was pulled over halfway. There was a pile of towels left on the floor near the bathtub, an open makeup case beside the sink and, on a key chain advertising the Fedora Café and Bar, next to a near-spent tube of Colgate, was a set of keys.

"Brian, Brian Bettman," he voiced a little louder, suddenly spotting a pair of legs poking through the shadows and lying awkwardly on the bed farthest away. When Bettman didn't say anything, the detective instinctively reached inside his trench coat, bumping into one of the hangers in the cubby next to him and knocking a denim jacket to the floor. Brushing his leg on the way down, it landed on his foot, startling him. At the same instant, he caught sight of the man's face and then his body leaning against the headboard in an unnatural pose with one arm hanging lifelessly over the bedside table.

Realizing in a heartbeat that Bettman was no longer of this earth, his open eyes staring off into space with a stone-cold, dismal solitude reserved for the hereafter, Lannigan kicked the coat away and then, satisfied he was alone, returned the .45 to its sheath. "It's an epidemic," he muttered, moving closer to the corpse. Staring at the dead man, trying to reconcile a connection and what it would mean to his client, the silence in the room became deafening as it crept under his skin, swirling about in his blood like a narcotic. He began to teeter. It was like a poison as he staggered backwards momentarily and, losing his balance, toppled into a chair by the desk, nearly falling to the floor, dazed. 'Ring around the rosy, pockets full of posies, ashes-ashes, we all fall down,' tiptoed eerily through his subconscious like a morose, medieval chant over and over again and rattling its essence, much like the tail of a snake preparing to lunge. All the while, he was nauseous as if he was hung over and contemplating the ring he'd found.

Suddenly thinking about the number of roses he'd sent to the chapel for Adella's funeral and who'd be next at the rate his life was deteriorating, gathering himself, the detective stood back up with his eyes fixed on Bettman. Even from where he was standing in the half-light, and in his condition, the cause of death was frighteningly apparent, being a hat trick in the man's neck and upper chest. Three bullets neatly placed. Quick and relatively painless, he thought, glancing around the room for any revealing signs that might offer more information than would the late occupant. As Mick walked past the end of the bed, he spotted a closed book of matches on the carpet. Snatching them up, he recognized the image on the outside. It was just like the key chain he'd seen, also promoting the Fedora Café and Bar in Kansas City, Missouri. Fiddling with the artsy cover and flipping it open, he discovered his name, 'Lannigan' scrawled on the inside, top flap along with his address, '2261 Palladin Drive, Apt. 222'.

From that he put two and two, and then two more together. Cognizant of not only where his client and the deceased man hailed from, but realizing as well his intruder was most likely the one who'd shot Bettman—and that Cassie could be implicated—he tucked the matchbook in his coat pocket. Then, leaving everything exactly the way it was, Mick carefully picked up Cassandra Carlisle's belongings, an untouched suitcase standing in front of the bureau along with the makeup bag and keys and, quickly sliding the luggage out into the hall, left the suite—wiping the prints off the handle of the door before closing it behind him.

Taking the stairs at the end of the corridor one floor down, he grabbed an elevator to the main lobby and exited the Plaza in no particular hurry, hoping that he'd avoid drawing attention to himself when Delray's finest asked later what who saw, when and 'are you sure it was Mick Lannigan carrying a suitcase and makeup bag?' 'Did he have a smoking gun and a guilty look on his face through the sweat pouring down it while you watched him skulk out of the lobby, or was he just woozy from the earlier blow to his head?' 'Claiming it was the door that changed his life and not opportunity knocking after all'.

Looking at all the things that seemed to be steering him in the wrong direction, it suddenly occurred to the man what he had left to accomplish in a day and a half if he could ever find the track to get back on it. It didn't look promising, he considered. Still, maybe Tiny could change that little detail and finally point him in the right direction or, at the very least, another one, more engaging; otherwise, his chances of success and survival were slim to none. And after conferring with the law, slim was already boarding a bus headed out of town...

Chapter 15

**Time and time, and time again, I'll choose 'this'
instead of 'that'. And as my luck climbs in the ring,
the upshot slams me to the mat. Yes, here or there,
forever foul or fair, the ride wields and winds its
weary way. While that fifty-fifty fate I face rears its
ugly head into the fray...**

—11:19 a.m.—

West 17th Street was an area of Delray most knew to
stay away from. That was true unless of course you were
unlucky enough to reside along the four-block corridor.
Grady Bascombe was one such individual. A short,
balding midget, dubbed Tiny, he made his living as a
busker up and down the squalid neighbourhood most
afternoons. He'd wander as far as his mind and legs
would take him, though always hoping to go further and
performing sleight-of-hand when he could afford the
tricks, or find an audience to confound. He panhandled
for loose change, flogging this and that when times were
lean, but the most lucrative income for the familiar
resident was selling hearsay: scandals, truths, half-
truths and lies and, on occasion, honest-to-God,

legitimate tips when the price was right and the information readily available. There was more than enough scuttlebutt to go around, he learned at a young age shortly after his father ran off on him and his mother only months before she was raped and killed, a few blocks from where he stood. As he'd told a friend, years earlier, the art of selling gossip was a lot like pandering and prostitution. The problem is it's only lucrative if there's a buyer interested in your tale. Thanks to Mick Lannigan, the man he'd shared that particular insight with, Tiny had managed to make a name for himself. It became a somewhat double-edged sword at times; however, appearances being the ultimate reference in man's flawed psyche, the rumourmonger, the fire-eating, sword-swallowing, card-carrying magician—who could pull almost anything out of a hat except a rabbit because he'd long since devoured it—was never much of a threat. And if he was well, like garbage on a Saturday night out in front of the West-Side cinema, he was easy enough to find.

After driving around in circles for nearly fifteen minutes and debating how he'd break the news to Cassie about Bettman when the time came, Lannigan pulled up beside a run-down greasy spoon. He was pleased to see his reason for being there, a charismatic little hustler who was huddled next to a fiery oil drum across the street on the corner of West 17th and Alameda.

It had been a while since the detective had visited the foreboding, little culvert of tenement row upon tenement row filling the skyline on both sides with aged and abandoned buildings, boarded up or falling down along the rat-infested strip of old-world neon and new age poverty. Following his last encounter, he'd told Doris it was the kind of place that had managed to successfully combine its wasteland of erotic foreplay with a demilitarized aftermath. Between the brothels and bars and the endless, adult video stores, off-colour magazine and smoke-shops, was a trailer-type restaurant. Down a block on the next corner, past a group of vagrants hovering about a liquor outlet like they were moths and it, the only light around, there was an out-of-place, out-of-the-way, stray gas bar. Its business would decline with the warmer weather and so to make due, there was a profitable, albeit illegal, casino flourishing in the back.

The look of it hadn't really changed much since the last time he'd needed to be there, thought Lannigan, spotting a hooker just up the street. A tall, long-legged early bird looking for a ripe worm he imagined, strutting her tail feathers and talons towards a lone driver beginning to slow up and roll down his window. The redhead leaned in, then stood up, removing a wad of gum and, smiling, tossed it to the ground with a flick of her hand. She walked around to the front of the rusted, black mustang, got in and, as soon as her door had closed, they sped away. Though, before it could disappear, Lannigan watched from the curb as another, a van this time, passed him going the other way.

Trolling for bottom feeders as well, he decided, giving in to the character of his surroundings and being that close to the gutter anyway, the detective stepped down off the sidewalk.

Crossing the street, watching the litter along the sidewalks swirling in the air and blowing around like urban tumbleweed, he saw Tiny going about his business, or one of them, flaunting his usual dishevelled appearance like a personal calling card. He wore a rumpled pair of blue jeans displaying a number of holes in the thighs of both legs, either frayed or fashionable, he couldn't tell. He had on a ragged, old, tweed sports coat over the top of a grey sweatshirt with its cuffs hanging out of the sleeves.

Standing there, as Mick studied the mini-magician in his fingerless wool gloves, it seemed he was only one bundle shy of a bindlestiff, though having nowhere to go, and his pronounced limp looked considerably worse since their last meeting.

All at once stopping, as if he knew he was being watched, and then smartly looking up, Grady Bascombe spotted an old acquaintance in the centre of the street. The man's trench coat fluttered briskly in a sudden, light but late April gust and he realized instantly it would be a better day than most, for him at least.

"Well if God should strike me dead, it's Mick, the *Irishman*," he yelled from the corner, using a Dublin drawl to make the tourist feel more at home. "Well, well, well, Brice Michael Lannigan his-self. How the hell is yah, gumshoe? It's been so long, I thought maybe you'd died... or given up on being 'the big dick' in this town," he stated, smiling and instantly reverting back to his natural patter.

"There *are* days, Tiny, and most of them have been this month," he confessed. "I see you haven't joined the circus yet," said Mick, extending a broad smile. "You're a natural with those shoes and that outfit. So tell me, what are you really up to these days?"

"About four-seven, I think, possibly eight this early in the day," he replied, drawing an antique, gold, pocket watch from his faded pants pocket. "Though I still don't buy into this shorter inches bullshit they're selling lately. Centimetres I think they call 'em." He grinned, winking up at the detective, already basking in anticipation and noting the outward semblance of his next customer. "Still one of the best straight men in town, but I gotta tell you straight up, Mick, you look like you've just been whacked by the business end of an eighteen-w... w... w... wheeler for Christ's sake. You look like shit! And that's giving you the best of it, no! On second thought, you'd have to look a whole lot b... b... better to look *that* good. What's up? We both know there's only one thing that would drag you down here, other than my graceful, good looks and that's good old reliable, tell-it-like-it-is, Tiny, with some real fine, timely, in its prime 'what-it-is' rap, am I right? I'm right, aren't I, Mickey? It's either that or you're here to give me a personal invite to your upcoming funeral, haha. So spill it PI guy, come on, what's the deal, as if I didn't know?"

"The way I'm feeling, I might have to flip a coin and get back to you," he admitted, pausing to stare up at a neon strobe flickering from the roof of a diner down the street, suddenly seeing his life flash before his eyes while he watched the light crackle, pop and then fizzle out of existence to join several others, leaving the sign to read as, 'The Lun—Bo-Di—'. Loosely translated from Mandarin Chinese, this meant, 'Rest in Peace' if his luck was holding out. "But in the meantime," he said, "I've got a hundred-dollar bill that talks even better than you, and it says *we* need to."

"What's your pleasure, the bank heist in Carmella? Unlikely, okay how about the suspicious blaze out in Delmonico? The real name of Danny, Fancy-Pants Fargus then, nah-uh-uh, that's a twenty-dollar trick. You know what I think? I think you're here to ask a few serious questions about something else altogether. Like maybe the death of Frank D'Angelo?"

"All right, I'm impressed. You just earned yourself a big, fat raise and doubled your money, Mr. Bascombe. Two hundred if I like what you have to say, say over lunch, on me."

"Lunch it is. You read my mind, what are you, psychic? I was just wondering where my next meal was going to be coming from. And not that I believe in all that mumbo-jumbo y'un-erstan', still and all, I had a premonition you might show up," he declared, sniffling

148

a bit and wiping his nose with the front of a sleeve. "Listen, Mick, and don't take this the wrong way or anything, but you don't mind if I see the little soldiers first? I mean, I trust you, you know that; but the word on the street is, you're so *broke*, you've been demoted to an art form. So tapped out," he went on, "the Bugle Corps hawked your horn." He hesitated, coughing. "By the way, sorry about your pal, Runyan. That was a bit of a double-header for you."

"Shit happens… all the time! You should know that about as well as anyone could," replied Mick, privy to the man's past and pulling out a handful of bills. "I just hope that what you have to tell me is a little more accurate, little big man. And while we're laying our cards on the table, and I don't mean those magic ones you play with up your sleeve, you are clean, aren't yah? Of this earth, I mean, because I sure as hell don't need you screwing with my head like you did the Bartleman case. You nearly got me killed with that bullshit you were throwing around!"

"Yeah, I still almost feel really bad about that." He laughed. "Don't worry," he said, his eyes bulging even bigger than normal through his wire-rimmed glasses at the sight of the detective's bankroll. "You'll get your money's worth. You got the 'Tiny' guarantee, and that's not as small as it sounds. You know me, only quality stuff, Mickey; after all, it's my *life*, right?"

"That's the thing, it's mine too this time," said Lannigan, shoving the wadded-up roll back into the

149

front pocket of his trousers. "So it better be; otherwise, this is the best either one of us will ever look." He paused. "And I think we both agree there's plenty of room for improvement."

"Not to worry, say isn't that yours, the Chrysler over there? I must be losing my touch, I heard it was stolen yesterday, but no, there it sits. Hmmm," said Tiny, noticing a pair of passers-by circling the silver sedan.

"I guess maybe you don't know everything, and somehow that's a bit more reassuring," Lannigan replied, looking back over his shoulder to see what Bascombe was so interested in.

"Or maybe I'm just getting ahead of myself." Tiny laughed as one of the men began jigging with the lock on the driver's side door.

"Hey!" shouted Lannigan. "Get the hell away from that you *sons-a-bitches*," he blared, drawing his .45 and presenting it to the car enthusiasts. "That's better," mumbled the detective and waiting a moment before putting the piece away. "Say listen, can I keep an eye on that from the diner?"

"Relax, they weren't shopping, they was admiring. I wouldn't worry… too much; besides, if you're willing to cough up two hundred dollars as easy as I seem to be coughing up phlegm, you have far more important things on your mind than cars. So follow me, these people over here …" he said, pointing to the diner, "… make the best friggin' burgers west of the Hudson,

Mick. It's the only reason I stay. I know I know, how sweet is *that* you're thinking, my lucky day, right? And I don't blame you, it's true. There's nothing like a damn good, quarter pound, lean and round, spiced and ground, one-inch thick mound of beef patty when you're talking turkey, I always say."

"You almost make it sound tempting, my very little friend. I'll be sure and tell all the right people about 'The Lun—Bo- Di—', especially the oriental ones. Obviously, the best kept secret on the face of the planet," remarked Lannigan, switching to a more serious tone. "Except possibly for the man who killed D'Angelo," he suggested, glancing back at the '95 Intrepid before entering the restaurant...

Chapter 16

On West 17th, it's not just what you know. It's about where you are, and maybe where not to go. And when strangers come calling who need answers and such, it's not the questions that matter, only why and how much...

—11.32 a.m.—

Inside the diner, Mick let Bascombe lead the way, watching the little man hobble down the closest aisle to an empty booth. Facing the street, past a jukebox mounted on the half wall, the two men sat down, listening to a piece by John Coltrane playing somewhere in the background, contending for a place amongst the smaze of cigarette smoke and the smell of grease.

"That's Maxwell Grogan over there with his back to us," said Bascombe. "He and his adorable wife, Lila, bought the place a million years ago when it was the 'Brown Bag' Dinette. How's that for a moniker? Talk about your accidents! It sounds like a collision between this poor little beggar and a damn, sissy Frenchman, so his first executive decision was coming up with a new name obviously. "The day he got the keys," he tittered, enjoying the coming anecdote even after all the times it had been told, "Grogan considered 'Maxwell's Silver Hammer', which explains the titanium colour you see everywhere. But common-sense prevailing over idle vanity, albeit a little late, especially since the words had nothing to do with food, well other than some residual morsel from his childhood, I suggested maybe he should just drop it like a 'hot potata'. Anyway, he said it was that comment that inspired him to come up with his *unbelievable*, garlic-pepper fries and jalapeño mash. He really didn't know what 'Silver Hammer' had to do with anything, haha. I told him it was a Beatle lyric about a mass murderer and, now that I think about it, who knows, the name might've caught on in these parts," he said, tapping the glass on the front of the jukebox.

"J-4 and he went with the 'Lunch Box Diner' instead, painted silver, excuse me, titanium from top to bottom, and the rest is history," declared Bascombe, looking past the counter and through a serving window into the kitchen.

"Hey, Maxey, a couple of your world-famous burgers over here stat, and with the works," he hollered, staring at the cook with his back still to them on the other side of the serving window. "And where's your beautiful, better half? You haven't misplaced her again, have you?" He laughed, looking around for the waitress.

"Make yourself comfortable, Tiny; she'll be out in two shakes and when I see the order, you'll see your meal, *stat*, and with the works," he said. "I'd ask who your friend is, but knowing you, you'd probably tell me, and more, and I don't think I really want to know," remarked the owner, sniggering as he looked out through the rectangular hole in the wall.

Seconds later, the door to the kitchen swung open. Creaking along to the musical tones of the jazz musician forever linked to H-2, Lila entered the room. Removing a pencil tucked stylishly behind her ear and seeming like it was a part of her permanent makeup, she headed straight for the unlikely-looking twosome occupying the booth nearest the door.

"You don't look like you're doing too well these days, Mr. Bascombe? And I'm not just referring to that cough of yours either. You will live long enough to tell me what I'm here to find out," asked Lannigan, smiling across the table.

"I'll live," declared Tiny, sharing a little coughing jag and dealing with a chronic tickle in his throat that had pestered him for days while he began sniffling some more. "At least till I take your money," he added, noticing the redhead out of the corner of his eye. "Hi sweet-cheeks," said Bascombe, gazing up at the woman as he leaned back. "This is Lila, Mick. Best damn waitress on 17th Street, possibly all of Delray." He paused, sniffling again. "And maybe even west of the Hudson River."

"Tiny, you're incorrigible, and don't you dare be slapping my ass again. Max doesn't like it." She winked. "So what can I get for you and your *friend*, here?" she asked, licking the tip of the pencil and then aiming it over the pad.

"You're in for a treat, Mick. We'll both have the same, Lila. Your old man's special and a couple of those tallboys, whatever's on tap is fine... Mick?" Mick shook his head; he was good with that. "And maybe you could sneak a few extra peppers on that plate for me," he suggested. "It's a little nippy out there this morning."

"Well there's certainly a *little nip* somewhere." She giggled. "I'll see what I can do about spicing up your life," she replied, slipping the pencil back where it came from, tucking the pad in her apron and going off to place the order.

"You do that every time you walk into the room, darlin'," he offered as she was leaving.

"I'll be back, boys," she said, smiling over her shoulder.

"That's fine, hon," replied Bascombe before looking across at the detective and considering the payday rather than the person he was staring at.

Listening to the exchange, Lannigan watched the diner suddenly begin to fill. The bell above the door behind them jingled nonstop as another, middle-aged couple walked in and sat down, leaving only a vacant stool or two at the front counter.

"Busy place," he said, glancing around the restaurant and pleased not to see any familiar faces. "So tell me, really, where the hell did you get that outfit,

Barbie's boyfriend? Who's dressing you these days, Charles Dickens?" Mick grinned, watching the owner's wife returning with the two blue-plate specials and getting more curious by the minute to find out just what Bascombe knew. Aware that, ordinarily, the man was so well informed, he could easily qualify for his own booth at a library and Lannigan was counting on the notion that this time it would be especially true.

"I'll have you know I bought this, all of it, off the rack. Right off the rack at Value Village in children's wear and they say kids aren't *good* for anything. No air miles a-course, but then I don't fly much if I have to leave the ground anyway, haha haha," he said, suddenly rasping, then hacking uncontrollably and reaching for a glass of water.

"Best burgers in the world you say," said Mick, starting to take a bite. Before Tiny could respond, Lannigan's throat felt like it was being raped and pillaged and set ablaze as he spit the mouthful back onto his plate. "What the hell is in *that?*" he barked, downing the full contents of his glass of water, quickly realizing it didn't do much except distract him a moment. He began gagging and coughing and, in short order, his headache returned worse than ever.

"Jalapeños," Tiny snickered. "You must have heard me ask for extra." He laughed, sputtering, choking back his own urge and trying not to follow the man's example. It would just be too pathetic he mused, watching Lannigan agonize over the sensation gripping the raw flesh inside his mouth and, all at once, feeling his throat begin to contract.

"Lila, could we get some milk over here for this tough guy in the trench coat, darlin'," he snorted, adjusting his glasses. "Yeah, the peppers are great for a cold. They really clean out your pipes. They'll clean out everything if you can get them down." He grinned.

"Well I'm Irish, you little *fart*," Mick grumbled in a scratchy voice, hanging onto his neck with one hand and awkwardly massaging it. "We don't eat spicy food for crying out loud and there's a reason for that, *hell*, we need a prescription for black pepper. You know for a wee man, you're the biggest son-of-a-bitch I know, you little smart-ass," he said, starting to grin. "Though it is the first time in almost five days I haven't wanted to shoot something for the wrong reason."

Lila appeared with a bowl of sour cream. "Go on, eat it," she said, handing him a spoon. He did and it worked. Almost immediately, he began to feel the fire burn out and the throbbing in his head subside.

"Twelve! Fourteen, Lila," shouted Grogan from the kitchen.

"Thanks, Red," said Bascombe as she went to cover the orders. "Hey, don't let it ruin your burger, take them off and give the little bastards to me," he said. "Oh and here's some more free advice more to the point, I suspect. It's about Fandano's son since I see you squirming at the bit over there, haha. D'Angelo met Adella Hughes at Conley International—"

157

"The airport, go on!"

"Yeah, and not even a week before the explosion. Anyway, I guess he charmed the pants off her," Bascombe explained, familiar with Lannigan's relationship with the girl. Sorry, Mick, but you knew he *was* a lady's man, right? I mean that was common knowledge, handsome as handsome goes, they tell me; certainly no match for you, or me." He smiled. "Independently wealthy and a built-in family of guardian angels watching over him; the guy had it all, and it still wasn't enough. I suppose when he saw the blonde, blue-eyed buxom beauty, he just saw what he *didn't* have and went after it, starting with a rendezvous at Adella's flat to pick her up that night."

"The night they were murdered, you mean? Which brings us to the big money question," declared the detective, reeling with expectations and anticipating a name or a lead of some kind, thereby extending his life a bit longer or, at the very least, until the next time fate turned its back on him.

"Yeah, the money," Tiny hesitated. "And do you know what else I'm sorry about?"

"No, what... what else could an unconscionable, little hustler like you possibly be sorry about?"

"That I've decided two hundred isn't enough, Mickey." He desisted looking out the window, debating the amount. "Yeah, I think I want five instead." Tiny coughed up, sneezing and wiping his nose.

"Five—" he barked. "Five hundred," he repeated, lowering his voice and eventually finding a normal volume. "What, you think I'm *made* of money, Bascombe?"

"I don't know what you're made of, Mick. I have an idea, but I think Fandano's going to find out for sure and pretty damn *soon* if what I hear is true," he whispered, leaning in and over the edge of the table.

"I guess there really is no honour among thieves, huh?"

"Why, you're not a thief, are you?" he replied, sitting back and grinning.

"All right you little, sawed-off pipsqueak, five then, but it had better be fact and not fiction this time! Who blew Fandano's kid up?" asked Lannigan. "Who wanted D'Angelo dead?"

Tiny looked back across the table and, sniffling, wiped his nose with a napkin this time, tossing it down next to his water glass. Clearing his throat and coughing several more times, he took another bite of his burger. Then eventually swallowing the mouthful, he replied. "My theory is that nobody in their right mind wanted him dead, Mick. I mean, think about it? Nah, I think you're asking the wrong question. Just like AIDS is God's way of saying, 'you fucked up boys'… you're going down the wrong path too, slick! He was never the target. You should be asking yourself who wanted Adella Hughes out of the picture," he insisted.

"Okay, so you think his death was an accident. Good on you! And like the thought hadn't crossed my mind. Answer the question, Bascombe, or don't you want this money?" he stated, hauling out five wrinkled soldiers and slapping them down next to his plate. "Now, quit stalling and wheedling your way around with stale friggin' theories and semantics, and just tell me who killed the two of them if you know, for Christ's sake!"

"That's just it, I don't, not exactly anyway," he mumbled, watching a stunned look wash over Lannigan's face. All at once, Tiny shared a delightful little smile before tearing into his Lunchbox burger and then quickly placing it back down. "It seems nobody does," he declared, still chewing, but unable to quell a hunger and sink his teeth into the man's money.

"Then what *do* you know…?" asked the detective, somewhat stumped by Bascombe's unexpected candour. Annoyed by his sheepish grin, he hoped whatever else the man had to say added up to a handful of soldiers and the price of lunch. "Because I'm in no mood for games, not today. I have neither the time nor the patience, even for your antics," he professed, the volume of his words gradually rising and getting sudden stares from around the room.

Changing his tone, and his voice above a whisper, Lannigan continued. "So what, if anything, *can* you tell me?"

"I know someone else who might," Bascombe replied, taking another mouthful, rubbing his nose and mouth on the sleeve of his jacket and staining it with some mustard.

"Okay," he said. "I can live with that as long as this someone lives in this time zone."

"They do."

"Look at me, Tiny," he ordered, waving his finger in Bascombe's face. "You'd better not be sending me on another one of your wild goose chases or my silent partner is going to have something to say about it."

"No, this is bona fide, top-of-the-line shit, Mick! No fooling," he replied, reading the intensity and desperation in Lannigan's eyes.

"Good, because if not, if it's the last thing I do, I'll come back here, find your sorry little ass and pop you right between those beady, little eyes of yours with a few loud remarks. And I'll do it long before Fandano's muscle catches up with me, I promise." He grimaced, watching the little man finally twitch.

"I get it! Okay! Her name is Katrina Goodhue," said Bascombe, giving up a tiny smile. "She used to trick-n-treat down this very strip as a matter of fact, years ago, until she moved out to Conley. That's where you'll find her, and when I say trick, I'm not talking magic, Mick, though some of her clients including this one right here …" he grinned, pointing at himself, "… used the term on occasion. You remember the 'Happy Hooker', don't you, slick, or are you too young and too strait-laced?" he asked watching the man barely shrug his shoulders. "Well anyway, around these parts, her parts gained her a reputation as the 'Heavenly Hooker'. Wily little kitten, A-1 prime, top-dollar toot *she* was. Man-o-man, even this fly-boy took a trip on those gossamer wings once or twice. And let me tell you, she was the silver lining behind a few dark clouds in those days," he admitted, taking pause and spotting his favourite waitress. "Now see what you've done; all that honesty gave me an appetite... hey, Lila, two more burgers, darlin'."

"Coming up, magic-man," she replied from across the room.

"Thanks, hon; you're the best!"

"Forget it, I'm done," announced Lannigan, throwing in the towel, a green and plaid napkin, onto a near empty plate.

"Not a problem then," he sniggered. "They're not *for* you."

"What are you trying to do, eat yourself out of a nickname?"

"Funny man, but I don't hear anybody laughing! Hey, the comedian's starving to death and in a restaurant no less," he remarked, scarfing down the last of his garlic-pepper fries. "You might want to quit talking all over me though; I'm trying to earn a living here," he said, eyeing the jukebox. "Say, you got two-bits?" he asked and watched Mick reach, reluctantly, into his trousers. He brought out a pocketful of change and tossed the handful down in front of him. The coins scattered, slid, spun, clanged and collided with dishes and one another. "Thanks," said Bascombe, taking only the quarter he needed. "Yeah, so anyway, this past winter, she hooked up with a guy I heard was doing more than just her. My grapevine says he's involved in a number of exploits, everything from small arms to extortion. Demilo I think his name was? Yeah that's it, *Vincent* Demilo, one nasty son-of-a-bitch too, a ticking time bomb. Completely unstable like a fricken volcano, ready to explode; do you like Blue Rodeo, Lannigan," he inquired, switching tracks and not missing a breath.

"I suppose, but do you think we could stay on topic? Though, why do you ask?" he replied, hoping perhaps it was leading somewhere meaningful. All at once he listened to the jukebox beside him whir, whine and rumble, lighting up like a carnival ride. After a momentary hush, the speakers began to crackle, pumping out 'Five Days in May'.

"Oh, I don't know, I just felt like playing a hunch," Bascombe said, grinning and taking a long drink from his tallboy. "Now, where was I? Oh yeah, she lives at eight one nine Delaware, apartment four one two. And when you see the platinum-blonde nymph, tell her Tiny says 'hi'," he added, smiling a sad little smile. Mick recognized the expression.

"Yeah, I can do that, but unlike you, no charge," he replied.

Shortly after that, Lannigan called the waitress over and, not needing a bill, handed her enough to cover their meal along with a very generous tip.

"Thanks, mister," said Lila, sounding surprised. "Come back anytime," she added.

"I hope that's an option," he remarked, considering his uncertain future while he watched Bascombe experience another one of his coughing sprees. Picking up the five hundred dollars, noting the anxious look of concern on the little man's little face, the detective slid out from the booth, listening to Jim Cuddy's voice winding down over the PA.

"What's the deal?" asked Tiny, wiping his nose. "That was worth *more* than five hundred," he insisted, staring at the money in Lannigan's hand—more than he'd seen in, he didn't know how long—and then looking up even further, locking eyes with the detective.

"You'll get no argument from me and, Grogan's right, you always say too much, but some of this was worth it, I hope," he stated, discreetly sliding the bills across the table at Bascombe. "Thanks, oh and keep the change. Who knows, you might just want to play another hunch after I'm gone," he suggested, giving up a grateful smile.

"Don't be a stranger, Mick," he replied as the detective began walking towards the door. The bell jingled while it closed behind him.

"Good luck," mumbled Bascombe under his breath. You'll need it, he thought; fanning the money out and staring at it awhile, he shoved the bills in a pocket and went back to the business at hand, lunch...

Part V

Chapter 17

Dealing with women is a complex demand, involving caring and closeness and ceding ground where you stand. It's more than body and spirit, or even heart, head and soul. Most often leaving one breathless or badgered to death and standing out in the cold...

—A HIGH-RISE IN CONLEY —1.45 p.m.—

Mick knocked on the door, hoping it wasn't the wild goose chase he envisioned and couldn't shake, hoping he wouldn't have to stick around too long to find out if it was or not and need to break in as a last recourse. It had been a few years, maybe even twenty or more since he was tested and tried, it's true he recalled, getting away with six months' probation and a hundred hours of community service for the juvenile felony. That was easy. The kick in the ass from his father, the resulting reprimands and his scathing condemnation right up to the time of his disappearance proved far worse than any sentence he could've served.

Sure, getting inside might save a little time in the long run, he speculated, examining the lock and sizing up the entrance with a gentle touch. Some things, you never forget. But what he really wanted was a hands-on with the lady of the house. After all, Katrina Goodhue was a professional and the only time he could do for it was with her, his curiosity—encouraged by the street urchin who'd led him down the primrose path to her fourth floor, garden gate—beginning to get the better of him. She knew which end was up and in his line of work, the end he was concerned with was the bottom-line involving answers and, for the moment, that was it.

He waited a second more, glancing up and down the well-kept, empty hallway. Quiet enough to hear a pin drop, thought Mick—admiring the thick shag underfoot—or maybe not, he smiled, rethinking the notion.

When there was no answer, he rapped again a little harder, his impatience pounding like a sounding board; like a silver hammer striking the back of someone's head if their name happened to be Joan, he pondered, detecting the irreverent chorus playing off an overactive memory synapse. 'Bang, bang! Maxwell's silver hammer came down upon her head. Clang! Clang! Maxwell's silver hammer made sure that she was dead.' And like a door slapping the back of his, the detective flinched, feeling it throb unexpectedly while he listened to the lyrics roll around one more time— 'Bang! Bang—'

"Who is it?" he heard a woman's voice reply with a drawn and uninterested tone.

"Mick Lannigan, Ms. Goodhue."

170

"I'm not expecting anyone …" she replied, hesitating an instant, "… at quarter-of-two. I don't have any appointments, go away!"

"If you'll just give me a minute," he insisted, "I'm sure I can change your mind."

"So, what is it you're selling?"

"I'm not selling anything, ma'am. The thing is I'm a private detective and a mutual friend told me that I'd find you here, at this address; I was wondering if you could spare a few moments of your valuable time?"

"A detective," she repeated.

"That's right."

After a prolonged and, to Mick's way of thinking, conspicuous silence, he heard the metallic clicks and clacking of latches, bolts and locks being worked and then, all at once, the door to number 412 opened a crack.

There, behind a security chain through a six-inch gap between door and jamb was an engaging woman in her mid-to-late thirties with shoulder length, platinum blonde hair. It was impeccable. She wore a tight-fitting pink blouse tied in a knot showing off most of her midriff and, farther north, an enchanting view of a delicate cross pendant dangling from her neckline. Besides a pair of shorts, the scant outfit included at least one stiletto heel on her visible foot, he noted, along with a doting, even passionate, smile rounding out more than her physical appearance when she looked up and saw the tall Irishman standing in the doorway.

Lannigan returned the gesture, sensing not only a rush of testosterone at the striking features of the beauty, but also that, perhaps, he was reading a bit too much into her greeting.

"Well, look what the Kat dragged in," purred the blonde with a playful stare while she undid the slide, letting the links fall before opening the door a little wider. It was easy to see Katrina Goodhue was intrigued, infatuated even, by the idea of getting acquainted with his unique breed, drawn to the legend and lore associated with the stimulating lifestyle she'd always imagined and all based solely on a love of old films. "Do you have some kind of identification?" she asked, recalling the line from a movie and reproducing the inflexions perfectly.

Lannigan removed his wallet from a back pocket under his coat and immediately flipped it open. "You are Katrina Goodhue, I take it?" he inquired, raising the open billfold, showing the woman his credentials, and likeness, up close and personal.

"That's right, I am," she replied, still scrutinizing the small, one by one picture. "You're far better looking in person, *and* much bigger," she added, grinning and studying the colour of his eyes. "And you're a real, live private dick, huh? So what kind... of questions, I mean?" asked the blonde, stroking him up and down with a furtive glance or two. Opening the door all the way, she shifted her eyes back to his momentarily, addressing the rugged looks of his chiselled profile under a burgeoning, noonday shadow and undressing the rest of him with her imagination while he put away his wallet.

"What kind?" he replied, embracing her lead. "I'm not going to lie to you, ma'am, hard, not *too* long, though I've no doubt you can handle whatever I come up with. In my business, except for a silent partner, it's the only tool I have. Questions, that is, but there's certainly no need to feel awkward or uncomfortable, I assure you. In fact, I'll do my best to make this little diversion as pleasant as possible for both of us. And the way things are shaping up, from my end anyway," he declared with an affable smile, "we shouldn't have any trouble at all making this work."

"Come in," she said in a soft, lurid and crescent pitch familiar to sailors and fans of Mae West. Forced to brush by her as he made his entrance, the detective could see all he needed with a quick glimpse of the one room flat, from the Murphy bed tucked away neatly in the wall behind him next to a bathroom, to the stereo system in a smoky, glass-encased maple wall unit surrounded on both sides by full-length mirrors. Both reflecting the back-splash of sunlight, and blinding at times in particular parts of the suite at certain hours of the day, he surmised.

Facing Mick was a window above the sink and part of a kitchenette with a small, round table and two chairs, all off to the side in front of a sliding balcony door. To his left, and past the suddenly attentive woman beginning to close the door in back of him, was an array of stock furniture. Nothing out of the ordinary with the exception of a bare bones computer in the corner that seemed completely wrong somehow sitting on top of an old, beat-up desk. Everything else looked current, right down to a uniquely crafted flower pot staring back at him with great, bulging eyes propped on a piece of Pier One wicker, and home for one lowly plant fighting for its life, decided the sleuth wielding his trained eye; he recognized the symptoms instantly, having been cursed with a black thumb himself. As well as a bizarre portrait hanging on the back wall, there were several mismatched tables scattered about, including one littered with Cosmopolitan magazines and a number of exotic travel guides.

"I was hoping to get a little background about someone you're supposed to be familiar with, a fellow by the name of Vincent Demilo."

"Vinny! What about him? I haven't seen that good-for-nothing two-face for weeks and when I do, believe me, he'll be one sorry ass if he shows either one of his faces around this place again."

"You don't say," he commented. "Okay, when was the last time you *did* see the good-for-nothing so and so?" asked Lannigan trying to accommodate her frame of mind and keep a straight face.

She hesitated a second, beginning to consider what the detective's presence actually meant. "What's this all about anyway? A woman, *I'll* bet?"

"In a way, murder ma'am; unfortunately, it's about a lot of things, but mostly… it's about murder. The Delray police haven't been able to solve it and my client wants to know, 'who done it', I guess you could say. Do you recall hearing anything about an explosion a few months back down in Ledbury? Two people, a man and a woman, were killed?"

"Maybe, I-I'm not sure. Who's this client of yours, anyone I might know?"

"It's unlikely, but it wouldn't matter anyway. I'm not at liberty to discuss that kind of detail. I'm sure you understand. Suffice it to say, a family member died and this *individual* would very much like to get to the bottom of it and, amongst other things, find out why it happened in the first place."

"And you think Vinny might be involved somehow?"

"I honestly don't know. This is probably a long shot, but it's the only one I have at the moment. That's why I come bearing questions," he submitted, looking around for anything suspicious. "So do you mind answering a few?"

"I hope that's not all you come baring." She grinned, twirling a locket of hair as she walked ahead of him.

"*Excuse* me, ma'am," he said following her, but not quite.

"Well, my time's as valuable as anyone else's," she replied, grabbing a pack of Marlboro off the counter and removing a cigarette. He considered the matches in his pocket from the hotel, but instead waited for Katrina Goodhue to light her own.

"Time, it's a valuable commodity indeed, I'm discovering. Do you mind if I sit down?"

"No, I don't mind," she said, feeling an unexpected tension in the air, taking a drag and immediately exhaling, taking another. "In fact, why don't you take your coat off and stay awhile, Mr. Lannigan."

"Thanks, I'm fine. Tell me, how long have you known this Vincent Demilo?"

"Off and on, I'd say a few years now. Ever since his marriage down in Missouri hit the skids and he left, right after his wife did." She giggled. "*Christ*, he hated that wench. She ripped his heart out and it drove him crazy for the longest time. This last come-round, he was more relaxed, for him anyway. He still has his moments though. At the best of times, he's stretched out tighter than piano wire."

"I don't suppose he ever mentioned anything unusual when you were together. Something that struck you as odd like say, God telling him he should build a space ark to save the population of Conley, or even Missouri?"

"A sense of humour, I like that." She paused, nibbling on the end of one of her fingers while the lengthy nail disappeared, watching him watch her. "Vinny couldn't build a house of *cards* if they were marked and his life depended on it. As for odd, there was a time back in January, maybe even February, I— I'm not sure any more, when he started drinking more than usual. Then he'd go on about how easy it was to make explosive devices with things lying around the house and just a little dynamite, or as he referred to it, 'dyna-fuckin-mite'. He talked about timers, caps, pipe, wires and all kinds of weird shit. It was to the point that I was almost as well informed as he was; but the whole time, it scared the *hell out of me* the way he went on and on about it."

"I can well imagine," said the detective, empathizing for appearances' sake, though not really having a clue how she felt. "It would scare the hell out of a lot of people," Mick went on, willing to say what she wanted to hear if only so she'd reciprocate. It wasn't wrong so much he thought, just accommodating for everyone involved. He did it all the time, he mused. No harm, no foul and she accepted the comments gratefully.

"Thanks." She wavered, all at once enjoying the deep blue of her caller's, wandering eyes. "Anyway, after a while he'd get on that box over there, interfacing I think they call it and spend hours doing God knows what till all hours of the day and night."

"On that computer, you say?"

"Yeah, sometimes I'd find him the next morning sprawled over the keyboard still passed out and it beeping and humming away like it was pissed off at the both of us."

"Do you know where he is now?" asked Mick, watching her lean against the counter, almost posing and watching him back.

"No idea. He could be anywhere. He comes and goes like an ill wind, like a sick and twisted, cold, ill wind. *Hell*, I might not see him again for another month, who knows. But if I was under oath, maybe tied and gagged ..." she said with a subtle smile from her indulgent, luscious lips and giving the impression she'd supply the necessary rope, "... and had to make a guess, I'd say he was in some grungy, little bar somewhere. With a drink in one hand, a slut in the other and a game going on, cards, you know?"

"I do, and speaking of cards, Tiny said to say 'hi'. Do you remember him at all?"

"Should I?"

"I can't say, but *he* thought you might. He sure remembers *you*, a midget about so high, little person if you believe in that politically correct bullshit. Personally, it's the kind of thing I try to avoid. He dabbles in this and that as well as a little magic on the side down along West 17th."

"West 17th Street, no, can't say as I do. The faces and names are all just a blur to me."

"Well anyway he uh, mentioned you were an entertainer of sorts yourself. An escort down there until you retired and moved out. Is that right?"

"Yeah an escort," she agreed, laughing. "Sure okay, a rose by any other, what is it, Mick, Mick right?"

"Right, well it's Brice actually, Brice Michael Lannigan but everyone just calls me Mick. I figure it has everything to do with the fact that I'm Irish." He grinned.

"You don't look Irish," the blonde admitted. "But your friend, Tiny, was right. I had to retire, Mick. I had to, and perhaps it was a blessing in disguise. Between my slap-happy pimp turned muscle-bound boob, the fucking johns giving me a run for their money and my landlord's fringe benefits eating into my profits, I was getting screwed for nothing most days!" she proclaimed, taking a long, deep draw off the cigarette. "I'm with a legitimate service now that eliminates the middleman." She winked at him, putting out her cigarette. "I like you, Mick, nice dimples and a cleft to die for," she sighed. "Does anyone ever call you Mickey? I'm sure they must," she said. "You're too adorable not to."

"Thanks," he replied, rubbing the stubble on his chin. "Close friends, sure, whatever you like, Ms. Goodhue."

"Kat, call me Kat, Mickey."

"Okay, Kat." Lannigan grinned, considering the countless innuendoes that came to mind before continuing his questions and, gazing at the clock on the wall, suddenly becoming obsessed with the time as well. "This fellow, Vinny, can you describe him to me?"

"No, not yet," she said. "You know what? I think a whole lot better with a drink in my hands, you know, when it's all that's available. Would you care to join me or are you in a hurry?" she asked, noticing him glance at the clock.

"Maybe I will... have a drink, that is."

"This is fifteen-year-old scotch, Mickey, and I save it for entertaining my *choice* clients if you see where I'm headed."

"I thought I did," he said. "So what's the going rate, would a fifty cover it?" he asked, taking one out and setting it down in front of her.

"Did I mention it was fifteen-year-old, *imported* scotch and that only the cream of the crop gets to sample the goods?" Mick didn't reply immediately, fumbling to switch gears, change lanes and keep up. "What's the matter, Kat got your tongue?"

"Not yet," he reported, smiling to himself. "And no, you didn't mention it, but now that I think I understand, let's make it an even hundred, shall we?" he suggested, matching the first bill.

"So you haven't told me, what does he look like, this Vinny character?" He repeated the question, watching the blonde fill up two shot glasses and then, setting the bottle down on the table, sat down herself.

"He's a big man, about six-five, bigger than you even, with these broad shoulders and huge, friggin' hands. Dark complexion, dark hair, dark everything, come to think of it, with green eyes and a beard," declared the blonde, taking a breath, debating what else to say and then giggling. "For another twenty, I'll even tell you the size of his—"

Lannigan interrupted her. "No, that won't be necessary," he acknowledged, smiling.

"—Mouse." She grinned, hesitating and batting her eyelids. "Other than that, I don't know what else you want to know."

"Whatever comes to mind, Kat. Mannerisms, habits acquaintances, anything you can think of."

She smiled. "I don't know that he has any acquaintances or male friends anyway. He knows plenty of women. Oh, and he has this irritating habit of talking to himself. It drives me nuts. He loves jewellery, gold necklaces, rings, big, gaudy ones with diamond chips, that kind of thing. He dresses extremely well. Usually in suits," she told him, remembering her chain. He gave me this," she offered, tilting her body in his direction and holding out an exquisite gold pendant. "One time though, I caught him trying on a pair of my nylons. Of course that doesn't help you at all unless you're planning to do a strip search." She laughed. "You're not planning anything like that now, are you, Mick?" She grinned.

"No," he said, smiling. She looked displeased for a moment and then went on.

"Listen, I can't make change, but I'm certainly willing to barter. I mean, I don't want you to think you're getting screwed here if you're not, so if you have any ideas," she said, locking eyes with the man briefly and, then moving around, leaning over behind him like a second skin.

"That's all right, Kat, really, I'm good."

"I'll *bet*," she whispered.

"Right, so if I get my answers, that'll be plenty, believe me."

"Are you sure?" she murmured brushing his face with the back of her supple, well-groomed hand, resting her frame over his back and breathing warmly into the nape of his neck.

"I know, how about instead of money, you take a ride down heaven's slide for the difference, then I wouldn't feel so guilty and Lord *knows* you'd feel better about things too, Mickey," she murmured in his ear. "What do you say to a little... Kat and mouse, mister?"

"Don't tempt me, gorgeous, not with those eyes and that smile, and—" he said, somewhat flustered, tripping over the thought and attempting to play the gentleman by changing the subject. "So then, is it serious with you and this guy, Demilo?" he asked as she meandered back and picked up her drink.

"Why, you jealous, Mr. Hard-headed *dick*, not-willing-to-give-an-inch?" she lamented, throwing back the contents of the glass, grabbing the bottle off the table and pouring another.

The detective desisted, smiling at the comment and, deciding it was a good time to do the same, downed his drink as well. Then when she leaned over to pour him another, her bosom all but falling out of the blouse, he denied the advance, covering the rim of the glass with his hand.

"We're just bang buddies. You know, fucking friends. We share a common interest, *me*," she confessed. "But I'm fast losing interest in the man's interest for me."

"I see," he acknowledged, appreciating the clarity of the terms and the apparently mature arrangement. "Then would you mind terribly if I borrowed something with his prints on it?"

"Not at all, how about these babies?" she replied, pulling down on the neckline of her middy and hoisting her bare breasts just inches from his face. "Will they do, Mickey?" she said, sharing a girlish grin. "He's had his hands all over them. Yes, no, what's your pleasure?"

"Well, the idea does give new meaning to the concept of hard evidence, I suppose. Still, I had something a little smaller in mind, not that those aren't," he stammered, "…you know, magnificent." He smiled, trying to focus. "However, I think I'd prefer something less conspicuous, like say a pen, some of his jewellery would be good or even a comb as long as it's personal," said the detective while she studied his eyes.

Pulling her top back up and adjusting herself, she picked up the lit Marlboro from the ashtray, walked over to the closet and took down an old, battered and bent Nike shoebox. When she returned, Katrina dumped it out all over the kitchen table. This is—" she began before he stopped her mid-sentence.

"All Vinny's stuff," he inquired, noting several interesting pieces including a collection of photographs, a ballpoint pen from the Ramada Inn and a soft-cover copy of *The Great Gatsby*.

"No, more of a catchall for a variety of keepsakes I couldn't come to get rid of for one reason or another. But you're mostly right, some of it's his."

"The pictures, what are they all about?" he asked, unable to make much from the unusual shots he was sifting through.

"Probably a trip I took to Coney Island, and maybe some old family photos; but there should be one in there of the two of us," said the blonde. "Yeah, there he is; that's *him*," she announced and pointed Demilo out at the entrance to one of the sideshows.

"Terrible likeness, didn't you say he had a beard though? This fellow only has a moustache."

"True, it's just been in the last month. Said he wanted 'to give the world a treat and try something new for a change'."

"I see," replied Lannigan, wishing he had a magnifying glass to get a better look at the man's features and suddenly thinking about an earlier conversation. "Do you believe everything happens for a reason, Kat?" he asked, combing through the remaining items on the table.

"I used to, yeah, but now I think everything happens just to make my life *more* miserable."

"Interesting, that's exactly how I felt till about three hours ago. But the trick isn't that three o'clock appointment you will or won't have tomorrow, or beating yourself up over something that happened, and that you had no control over, or even Tiny pulling a rubber chicken out of a hat because he can't afford to feed a live rabbit; the trick is to reconcile the reasons why. To figure out the connection," he voiced as if a moment of revelation. "And then everything is right again, at least for a while," he added, his tone dropping as his eyes fell on the book lying on the table. "Do you mind if I hang on to this?" said Mick, lifting up the cover, looking for addresses, names or clues, but finding none.

"Sure, call it change," said Kat. "You don't seem to care for *my* currency."

Ignoring the comment as a simple tactic of self-preservation, not wishing to walk directly into an active landmine, he pressed on, taking another overland route altogether.

"Maybe it's not my place, but isn't your relationship with this guy, Demilo, a bit strained and unorthodox? It seems to me women don't do much, if anything, without a reason," said Lannigan. She didn't answer right away, lighting up another cigarette.

"Then I guess I must've had one," she replied.

"I guess," he agreed, not inclined to pursue the basis for their attraction—satisfied it was nothing more than that, and for what it was worth, cognizant that her remark was past tense. "So do you use the computer, gorgeous?" he inquired, seeing it as the square, plastic and metal peg in a big oak board full of round holes.

"No, never, he brought it home one day just after Christmas."

"Vinny, you mean?"

"Yeah, he said the store was practically giving them away. Like I said, he sure spent a lot of time on that contraption. Although I don't believe I've seen him near it for months now, and now it just sits there collecting dust."

"May I?" asked Lannigan, pointing to it and already beginning to get up.

"Sure, be my guest, but I don't know if it even works. Maybe that's why he hasn't been using it." She huffed pouring another drink for herself, with the rouge-stained cigarette dangling between her lips.

Lannigan sat down in front of the computer screen, turned it on and it worked. It worked just fine. Slow he determined, but obliging nonetheless and complying with his every command as long as he was willing to be patient.

He checked the files and, along with a jar full of cookies stored in memory, he also found a number of notable bookmarks. Sites like www.kaboom.com, www.skyhigh.com, swedish.bombshell.nl and www.pipedreams&alarmclocks.com. He reviewed the history file of the user and there was only one listed, under a Lonzo Ricciardi. Not Vincent Demilo to his surprise. The name Ricciardi meant nothing to him, but then neither did Vincent Demilo before he walked through Kat's apartment door. The files documented websites visited dating back nearly four months to the sixth of February in one instance. It linked the user to a site called 'Build-a-Better-Bomb'. He didn't know what the connection was between the two men, but he'd capture as much of the information as he could and forward it to a friend at the 52nd Precinct since he owned neither an email address nor a computer. Making his own connection, he copied the history to an email and attached two other documents buried in sub-directories under his name/personal/research/C4/.

To: jgarrett@52precinct.com
Cc:

Subject: History File 819 Delaware, Apt. 412 for Vincent Demilo (Lonzo Ricciardi)?

Jimbo,

I don't have time to explain, but I'd appreciate it if you could file this away for safekeeping just in case I ever need it. There's some good shit here and I can't really walk out with a computer under my arm.

Thanks, Mick…

PS: See you in a few hours.

"Do you have a phone book handy, Kat?" he asked, still facing the monitor and typing away, busy gathering, and transferring, a collection of personal files, including a batch of cookies he'd located that were every bit as good as footprints in the sand or fingerprints on a book. Satisfied he'd stripped it of all he needed, the detective sent his message and then seeing the confirmation, turned off the machine. He turned around and the blonde immediately handed him the Conley phone book.

Flipping through it, looking for outlets in the area in the business of selling explosives and finding only four, he quickly tore out the page, folded it up with his one free hand and shoved the paper in his coat pocket.

"Well, that's about all the damage I can do here, gorgeous," he confessed, setting the phone book down next to the computer. "I'll just be on my way so you can get back to whatever it was you were doing before I disturbed your day off."

"Are you sure you can't stay just a little longer now that your business is out of the way? You're far more interesting than painting nails or drinking alone would be, and we really never did get around to well, get around to asking questions about me, Mr. Detective," she said, rubbing up against him and gently caressing his chin with a long, white-nailed finger or two.

"Maybe some other time, but it's been a slice of heaven as they say on 17th Street," he grinned. "You're a delight, Kat," he stated, following her to the door and not wasting the view.

"You're welcome, and remember," she murmured. "I *have* the reason if you ever need a place, Mick.

Anytime," she purred, leaning into the door, holding it open and juxtaposed so, causing her breasts to collide with one another. Two mounds formed a perfect cleavage, consuming the pendant and leaving only the fine, gold chain visible as he went by her into the hall, unable to avert his stare from the milky-white chasm of the heavenly body, as if, suddenly, a black hole swallowing up his runaway thoughts along with both eyes whole.

"*Anytime* is it? I'll keep that in mind. It's quite likely my favourite time by the way," he said, all at once wanting to test his gossamer wings and pulling her to him, kissing the blonde, long and hard just for the hell of it just then, just in case, "Thanks, gorgeous, oh, and one more thing."

"Name it," she said eagerly, embracing the sensation of his lips on hers.

"I'd consider it a personal favour if you kept this tryst our little secret," said Lannigan with a quiet smile. Winking at the blonde and considering what might be possible if he had a few hours, then tightening the belt on his trench coat from years of habit, he tucked his hands inside the pockets, admiring her features one last time.

"As long as you promise to introduce me to Mickey's *mouse*, mister, the next time you're both in town," she whispered, sharing a naughty smile and catching his eye. As he watched her ever so slowly close the door, realizing his headache had vanished and that he'd gotten what he needed and more, all the detective could do was grin. At the same time, he was also aware that the entire time he'd been with Kat, he hadn't thought about Cassandra Carlisle one time. On the other hand, Doris's voice on the answering machine nagged at him, and more than once…

Chapter 18

The right to bear arms doesn't mean wearing less or 'short sleeved'. Perhaps rolling them up as the general public's deceived? Its intent wasn't ever to fire on 'their own kind', but rather on armies invading from beyond enemy lines. Distorted and twisted, the loaded die was pre-cast for blazing a trail on the blood of the past...

—2.40 p.m.—

According to the cluster of advertisements on the page that Lannigan had taken from Katrina's phone book, and subsequently from his coat pocket, there were only four gun shops, in all of Conley. Of those, three were in the business of selling explosives: 'Bang for the Buck', 'Round the Corner Eastside Armoury' and 'Shoot for the Stars Emporium'. The fourth, 'The Gunrunner', he eliminated since it was strictly small calibre firearms, rifles and ammunition.

Pulling up in front of the 'Eastside Armoury', he shut the car off and took his keys from the ignition; though rather than getting out, he found himself leaning over the steering wheel, staring off into the early afternoon and contemplating Doris's message once more. Something she'd said bothered him, though he couldn't quite put his finger on it.

Setting the elusive notion aside, the detective got out, bought a half-hour on the parking meter and went in. The shop wasn't busy. Seeing only one other customer wandering the aisles in a flak jacket and military boots near the back facing the entrance, Lannigan spotted a salesman standing behind the counter. He was stocking a display shelf as the detective approached.

"Say," said Mick, gaining his attention almost instantly. "I notice you don't have any statues of Charlton Heston around anywhere. Isn't that sacrilegious or some kind of blasphemy? I thought he was the Patron Saint of Arms and Ammunition." He smiled, nonchalantly picking up a plastic container of unknown, white liquid. "Aren't you the least bit concerned he'll be offended, come down here and smite you with a backhand from God? Or could it be you're just in it for the money and not a disciple at all? Only *selling* violence and not preaching the word to peace-loving Christians," suggested Lannigan, glancing at the label on the bottle of gun cleaner before putting it back down.

"Hahha, Heston, cool, the NRA, I *get it*! Yeah sure, CNN, the Learning Channel, right," said the gangly clerk with stringy, shoulder length black hair, beginning to look anxious. He assisted his speak with one overactive hand, contorting it into an unrecognizable mass of writhing digits as he continued to express himself to the man staring back at him. "Yeah, pretty much the money, and like Moses would ever stop in here to check *me* out, hahahah!" said the shopkeeper. "Or 'pry this weapon from my cold, dead hands', haha. Let him *try*," said the fellow, stroking a favourite target pistol before placing the Browning semi-automatic Challenger back in its case. "Thanks, mister, that felt good," he said with a smile, stroking more than just the merchandise.

If you liked that, *wait, there's more* thought Mick, eyeing the weapon under glass, reminiscent of a P-08 Luger, nine millimetre eight-round semi his father owned.

"Nice piece," remarked Lannigan, noting a hint of gunpowder in the air.

"It's a collector's item these days. This model's been discontinued for, about thirty years now, I'd say. It's our last one. Awesome barrel, sleek and slender with a fully adjustable back sight mounted on the half-length slide. The grip is sweet, isn't it? That's pure walnut, with a great feel and more like velvet than wood; .22 calibre, superb point-ability, the trigger pull is totally adaptable as well and the whole piece, chrome-plated. Go ahead… make me an offer, mister? By the way, we're having a storewide sale this month on handguns, this one included if I don't snatch her up first." He laughed. "You buy it and we'll fill it for free.

That's a forty-dollar saving on the first magazine, not a bad deal, huh? And you look like a man who knows his way around the business end of a barrel. What do you say? Anything in the shop from Buntlines to bazookas and Colts to cannons, no imports though." He hesitated. "That was for the benefit of old man, Moses," stated the clerk, winking at the customer. "Interested?"

"Not really, no. I admit it does sound tempting, but I'm here on other business. Lieutenant Lannigan with the FDA," he announced, suddenly sounding curt, far more reserved and hauling out his wallet, flipping it open. Then flopping it closed even more quickly, he tucked the prop back in his pocket before the fellow could see anything but a blurred picture and a city seal declaring that he was a recognized officer of the law.

"I've been keeping an eye on this establishment for a couple of weeks now, son." Mick hesitated intentionally, exhibiting a serious glare and a dire tone. "And I have to tell you, there's a whole lot you're not doing by the book around this place. Still, maybe we can clear up some of those, concerns. Then I won't need to write a book on you for the six or *seven* flagrant counts of mismanagement, negligence and possible criminal behaviour that I've documented—and some of it on tape. As a matter of fact, I'm having a sale of my own today, 'no charge', felony or otherwise." He grinned. "What do you think, Ryan Denton?" asked Lannigan, reading the name tag on his olive drab, army fatigues. "I'll forgo my usual report if you're willing to give me access to your register for five or ten minutes. I'll even forget about the infractions for false—"

"Hey… wait just a second, I know my—"

"Uh-uh-uh," said the detective raising his hand to avert the salesclerk's claim. "You know your what, your rights under the Fifth Amendment? The sentence for aiding and abetting a deranged psychopath, is that what you know, Mr. Denton? Well, just for the record, let me tell you what I know. I know all you have to do is *cooperate*," he asserted, taking pause at the man's discouraged expression. "Don't make me slap you with a friggin' fine or worse, so many restrictions and violations on this place that by the time you get out from under the pile of shit they refer to as red tape down at City Hall, guns will be extinct. And this store, just like you, will become a distant memory. But I'm a decent guy, so I'm willing to overlook your personal involvement with a known terrorist, not to mention accessory to murder. Again, no charge! *Hey*, maybe you *didn't* know." He desisted, giving the man another minute to consider his options. "Now, you were saying?"

"I was saying, no problem, what is it you'd like to know?" replied the clerk.

"I want to know if a man by the name of Vincent Demilo, or possibly Lonzo Ricciardi, purchased any kind of C-4 explosives from you in the last three months."

"The last three months, I'll have to get the records in the back. Hang on," he said, entering the rear of the shop through a swinging door.

Less than a minute later, Denton reappeared empty-handed. "We did a spring cleanup last month. All of our records were sent to the warehouse. The building's down on Bayswater. It'll take at least an hour to get them over here," he said, staring back at the trench coat from across the counter, nervously biting his lip.

"I'm afraid you don't have an hour, son. I have places to go. Reports to write and people to bust, so what I will give you is twenty minutes, starting *now*. I'm going across the street to get a cup of coffee and be back in twenty-one minutes. Are you clear on that or am I mumbling again?" Denton shook his head and reached for the phone before Lannigan could even turn to leave.

Less than twenty minutes later, Mick Lannigan walked back across busy 2nd Avenue to find what he needed waiting for him on the counter. "It took some doing, but that's everything you asked for."

Lannigan glanced at the clerk, smiled and directed his eyes back to the book. "This is your only register for the last three months?"

"That's it," he said, "everything! If you don't find what you're looking for in there, we didn't sell it to the guy you're after."

Mick opened the leather-bound chronicle back to February and began skimming forward through the pages of items, dates and customers. Finding nothing under either name, he continued his search well into the ides of March after the day of the explosion, before finally slamming the book shut. "I guess what I'm looking for is somewhere else. Round another corner maybe," he said, turning to leave and, adjusting his fedora to the front of his brow, quietly walked away. At the same time, double guessing his instincts and debating whether he was even on the right track or not, Lannigan stepped outside into a sudden, cool breeze as a light drizzle began to darken the sidewalk and threaten flurries.

"*You're welcome*," shouted the clerk, watching the door close behind him.

Flipping up his collar and then removing the sheet of paper from his coat pocket, the detective looked at the next stop on his list, 'Bang for the Buck', ten blocks away on Lakeshore Boulevard. Getting in and driving off, he found himself gazing in the rear-view mirror feeling like he was being followed.

***

"Good afternoon, I'm looking for the owner," said Lannigan to the fellow in front of him ringing up a sale.

"I'm the owner," he replied, handing the customer his change. Picking up his parcel, the shaggy-haired member of the 'Cruisers'—according to the embroidery stitched on the back of his sleeveless vest—left. "I'm the manager, cashier, clerk, bookkeeper, chief cook and bottle-washer, a janitor on occasion and security when the situation calls for it."

"That's fine, the owner will do. So why don't you give the rest of your staff the afternoon off." Instead of smiling back, the man at the cash register looked at his watch. "Anyway, the name is Lannigan. I'm with the FDA," he said, getting a sense that time was an issue for the gentleman. "We're conducting an investigation in and around Conley. Talking to all of the shop owners." He paused, glancing around the store. "Like yourself. We think that some C-4 purchased from this or one of the other local outlets was used in what turned out to be a double homicide over in Delray. I'd like to take a look at your register if I could, and maybe ask you a few questions about your clientele," said the detective, showing the owner his identification.

"Say, that's not a badge and it doesn't say anything about the FDA. What's going on here, mister?" asked the gentleman with an uncomfortable and puzzled look. "Who are you?"

"Relax, sir. My name *really is* Lannigan, but you're right. The FDA doesn't use badges, never have and probably never will. You should know that unless this is your first store audit, or perhaps you're not who you say you are," suggested the detective.

"It is and I am," he replied. "I've been in business for just about a year now. I keep my nose clean and I run a legitimate enterprise, fellow."

"Whoa, ease up. No one's disputing it, sir. We're not questioning your integrity, just looking for a few answers and a little cooperation is all. And as for the ID, I was only hired by the agency earlier this week as an investigative consultant, but if you'd like, you can certainly call my superior? I'm sure he can put an end to any doubts you might have and confirm who I am."

"You know what? That's a damn good idea, I think I will! What's his number?" asked the owner, hastily grabbing the receiver.

"Five five five, six four five three, the commissioner's name is Garrett, Mr. James Garrett. The clerk dialled and waited while it rang three or four times.

"Garrett," said the voice at the other end of the line as soon as he picked up.

"Mr. James Garrett?" asked the clerk, staring back at Lannigan, not willing to take his eyes off the man in the trench coat till he got some answers of his own.

"Yes, and you are?"

"I'm calling from the 'Bang for the Buck' gun shop on Lakeshore. I have someone here who says he works for you people at the FDA.

"Put him on, would you, Mister?"

"Ridley."

"Mr. Ridley, right. Thanks."

"He wants to speak to you," said the owner. Mick reached for the phone even before it was handed to him.

"Chief, yeah, this is Lannigan. Listen, I drew a blank at the Eastside Armoury a little while—"

"What the hell are you pulling now, Mick, and why are you dragging me into these ridiculous games of yours?" inquired his oldest friend.

"Well, that's right. I had no choice, Mr. Garrett. So far, extremely cooperative, there was just that slight misunderstanding about my credentials. I mentioned to your personnel that it might be a problem, anyway, sorry to bother you like this. I know you're a busy man, but at least everything's under control, right?" said the detective, eyeing the clerk and smiling. "Yes, as soon as I find out anything, I'll report back to headquarters, right, to you directly, got it! Yes, sir!"

"Lannigan, one of these days you're going to cost me my job and when you do—" Garrett went on as Mick reached over and hung up the phone.

"Now where were we? Right, I'm looking for a man who was in here three or four months back, buying explosives around February."

"Look, Mr. Lannigan, as much as I'd like to help, its closing time and my hours are seven a.m. till three p.m. It's five after now. I got a kid to pick up at school and I can't remember who came in here three or four hours ago, let alone three or four months.

"That's why you keep a register, isn't it, Mr. Ridley? You heard my boss. I will have to take a look at it. I'm sure it won't take long."

"Come on, man, the register's locked up in a safe in the other room. And tomorrow's another day," he argued.

"Not for some people it isn't, for some of us, today is it; so are you going to let me see your records or not? Five minutes and I leave with a glowing report for *you* and your little corner of the gun trade, and hopefully with the evidence I need in my pocket. Or do I stand here until you show me what I want to see, and the glowing report becomes a negative submission to the licensing review panel? It's your call, Ridley."

Without a word, the middle-aged man reached around in back, pulled out his register and placed it on the counter in front of Lannigan. Opening the large, brown leather-covered book to the month in question, he immediately spun it around for the investigator to look at. "Make it quick! *Please.*"

"I'll do my best, but lately that's not so good," he confessed, bending over to examine the contents. "I thought there were strict regulations about selling these materials?"

"There are, and the man must've had a proper permit, otherwise I wouldn't have sold it to him, that's all I know. I'm not going to lose my licence over something like that."

"What about forgeries?" inquired the detective, his eyes suddenly jumping off the page after spotting the name of Demilo near the bottom of it. "Here it is.

Finally, February twenty-second, Vincent Demilo. But what's this?" asked Lannigan, "Dannello?"

"Probably the name of his company, and there, there's the permit number next to the date, number D as in Demilo, zero twenty, two zero four slash zero zero nine. The 'D' signifies it's a construction permit issued by the city." He paused. "Two kilos: that doesn't seem like much for a company," he said.

"Do you remember asking him about it?"

"No, but then I don't remember what I had for breakfast either."

"I don't suppose you recall what he looked like then?"

The man shrugged his shoulders. "In ten minutes, I won't remember what *you* looked like. So are we done here?"

"I'd say that's a big yes, but I will need a copy of this page with *his* signature, and the receipt."

"Fine," said the shopkeeper, sounding put out. "But if my son isn't there waiting for me, I'm going to sue the ass off the whole damn FDA, starting with yours," he mumbled under his breath, disappearing in the back, lugging the book with him...

Chapter 19

Friends are who we count on to help us get from here to there. Whether it's the coldest night, the darkest day or whether weather's foul or fair. When tethers have been tested, limits reached and boundaries crossed, without a shoulder or a willing hand, it's safe to say much would be lost...

—4.27 p.m.—

On his way back to Delray to see a friend at the 52nd Precinct—and there weren't many—Mick couldn't help but wonder what Demilo had to do with Adella Hughes or Frank D'Angelo, if anything at all. Yet, just like Bascombe, his instincts told him otherwise. The only connection he had, no matter how much C-4 the man bought, was the matchbook from Bettman's hotel room and the fact that Demilo seemed to be living in Missouri off and on since before his marriage fizzled out. Still, if the prints on the book were to somehow match the matchbook from the 'Fedora Café and Bar', he'd certainly have something—but *what?* And how was it possible, he mused? It would be like pulling a much-needed needle out of a haystack that you weren't even looking for to begin with and, all at once, he was aware of what had bothered him about his secretary's message. 'There was a suspicious-looking character watching us as we downed a cab near the Mayflower', Doris mentioned. 'Cassandra said he seemed familiar.' Then the more he thought about the likelihood, the more he realized it meant the guy who busted into his apartment that morning and sent his day into a time-lapsed tailspin could very well have been Vincent Demilo himself, as well as the man who choreographed the explosion and Cassandra Carlisle's husband, he debated. Overwhelmed by the revelation, he turned onto Riverside a block from the station house. And if so, was D'Angelo the intended victim all along, making the girl the innocent in all of it? Between the merry-go-round of ideas parading in and out like a chorus line of freak shows at the Big Top and the headache that had returned leading the way, Lannigan pulled over, turned off the car and closed his eyes for a few minutes. Afraid he might pass out if he stayed where he was too much longer, the detective sat up and reached for the door handle.

Entering the precinct, he hurried down the hall to the office of his long-time mate, Jim Garrett. Not bothering to knock, Mick went in, pulled the door closed and sat down in a steel-framed chair obviously intended to deter visitors from staying long.

"Well, aren't I the fortunate one? If it isn't special agent Lannigan from the FDA, oh yeah! Thanks for hanging up, because I'd run out of expletives. Come to think of it, I can catch up now," said Garrett from behind his desk.

"I admit, it sounds like fun, but I don't have time, maybe later. Right now, I need your help, Jim."

"That's rich." Garrett snickered. "You force me to impersonate an officer of the FDA, make me do a little dance with this fellow till I figure out what the hell is going on and then you slam the phone down in my ear. And wait a minute, if that's not enough, you show up at my place of work, plop yourself down and ask me to what, pull your ass out of the fire… yet again! Have you considered calling Guinness about the size of your balls, Mick? I think they might be interested! Lord knows you could give them a run for the record." He paused, studying the man in the trench coat whom he'd seen look better the morning after the night before than he did at that moment. "You look like shit, Mick!"

"Then I should feel as good as I look," he replied, slouching back in the chair trying to get comfortable.

"I already know what you're going to ask, but Stern is my boss and his cases are confidential, you know that."

"Come on, Jim, to hell with Stern. Shit, you and I go all the way back to pre-school for crying out loud," he remarked, recognizing the by-the-book look on his friend's face. "You're not going to tell me that a, literally, small-time hustler and a swanky, hot-to-trot hooker are willing to give me a hand, *amongst other things,* but you, my oldest friend in the fuckin' world can't be bothered to show me the time of day? No fooling, Jimbo, it's serious this time. Now what? *What?* Are you still sore about the phone call?"

"No, but he'd have my head if he ever found out, and when I say 'my head', I don't mean the one you see sitting on my neck here." Garrett hesitated, sensing desperation in Lannigan's voice he wasn't used to hearing too often. "How serious anyway? *What...* does he have a case?"

"Don't be asinine; of course not. Would I be sitting here in a police station if he did, and especially this one? But what's the difference how serious?" said Mick. Besides, if I ever told you, he mused, and considering it, you'd never believe me anyway. "If I say it's serious, Jim, you know I'm not screwing around. All that matters is I need your help, a lousy favour for God's sake, and that should be enough. Okay maybe a couple, three or four tops. Is that really so much to ask after what we've been through?" he submitted. "Look, Stern isn't worth this kind of aggravation, neither is this job. *Hell,* I'll give you a better one if I can survive the next day or so in one piece."

"That's great, Mickey, but I'm not even sure you're really employed," said Jim, grinning at the man.

"I must be, I caught myself chasing my own tail a couple of times this week already, so what do you say, Jimmy, it's me over here... a line, throw me a rope."

There was a short, awkward silence and an anxious moment or two. "So what are you not saying then, no?"

Garrett only stared back, contemplating a wife, two kids and a daughter who was struggling with multiple sclerosis while he struggled with all that carried with it.

"That's fine, but just so you know, you're probably the only person in the world that can point me in the right direction, and all I'm asking for is a few lousy answers and a bit of your precious time. Call it payback if you like, beginning with who took the rap for you back in grade school when you glued Miss Haliburton's skirt to her chair. Do you remember? That was the day we discovered black garter belts, sheer nylons and a true appreciation for the female thigh first hand, haha." Even Garrett chuckled under his breath. "You should be thanking me for your jumpstart in the field of sex education. And who was it that helped you out of a jam in high school on prom night when those two fucking bikers the size of trucks were going to kick the shit out of you after they drop-kicked your ass through the uprights? I forget now, remind me. Exactly who was it that took three broken ribs, a concussion and forty-five stitches, and who was it got the cheerleader after somebody else was checked into Eastside Memorial for observation? Say, stop me when you begin to feel even a twinge of guilt, or just the least bit grateful, Jimmy." He paused, giving the man a chance to step up. When he didn't, only swivelling from side to side in his chair looking out the window, Mick continued. "All right, then how about the time I confessed to your mother that the magazines she found under your bed were—"

"Okay already, enough. All right, goddamn it! You made your point!"

"That's better, that's the Jimbo I know, appreciate and love… to abuse." He laughed.

"What's this favour then? Or should I say… favours?"

"A book of matches and it's a long story, but I'm not going to bore you with the details, mostly because I don't have time and don't know most of them anyway, which is why I need you to check it for prints. My hunch is they belong to a fellow by the name of Pilattzi, Antelo Pilattzi, sorry, that's his name. I also need you to compare this book for prints as well …" he said, pulling the soft-cover from an inside coat pocket, "and run a check on possible priors. Apparently, he's a nasty piece of work on his good days, so there should be something on the man, somewhere. And last but, by no means easiest, I'd like you to trace the plates on a red Grand Prix, late model I figure, licence number, XD."

"That's it! That's what you're giving me, 'XD'?"

"Well no, of course that's not all. I also think it's a rental," said Lannigan, smiling.

"A rental, this helps somehow? You know this'll take time. I can't just snap my fingers if all you're going to give me is two letters, a colour and a hunch. I'll have to get back to you."

"You can't, I don't know where I'm going to be. When do you think you'll have something?"

"End of day maybe."

"Can you do better? Like I said, I'm kind of pressed for time."

"I'll see what I can do, Mick."

"I'll call you," he said.

"So what's the other thing, you said four?"

"Yeah, some inside information on Stern's case, so besides me what do we have to go on?" He grinned.

"It's true, isn't it?" replied Garrett. "As long as I can remember, trouble has come looking for you. Even if it was somebody else's, you were odds-on-favourite anyway. I guess some things never change." His long-time friend took a file from his cabinet. "Well, excluding yourself, rumour has it that the 'Brayside Bomber' might be involved. Stern figures one of two possibilities: this guy instigated the whole thing on his own for whatever reason right up to and including payback and revenge maybe, or the owner of the building hired him for the insurance. Either way, it seems Dunvega banked every penny of his winnings no matter which side you choose. Given that scenario, that would make Adella and the other fellow innocent bystanders. But like I said, that's the spin that Stern put on it. Oh yeah, footnote, Abitibi paid up in record time, but that could be fortuitous as they say in the business."

"That's good, what else, Jim?"

"Well, and you're not going to like this, but suicide still hasn't been completely ruled out apparently from what the lieutenant is saying. You know, due to a history of depression and—"

"And what, that's crazy! Why would anyone commit suicide by blowing themselves sky high, particularly a girl who was frightened to death of firecrackers and loud noises? That's nuts!"

"That's Stern, but it's not an argument, Mick."

"I know, still, does he think she used the stuff to get over her fear of… just before." He stumbled and just as quickly, regained his footing. "It *was* C-4 that was used—right Jim?"

"That's what the file says, but to be honest, I couldn't tell C-4 from KY Jelly or ABC gum." He laughed.

"None of it makes any sense. Did somebody up his medication for *Christ's sake*?"

"Talk to him," he replied. "I only work for the man, I'm not his keeper. On the other hand, there is this husband angle, ex-husband actually, Tony Scalatto. He made two calls to Adella a couple of weeks before her death."

"Scalatto, that's perfect! You just saved me a call to the Hall of Records in Missouri. So give, where did he call her from?"

"The first time was from Kansas City and the second, just up the street you might say, over in Conley," he reported, putting the file down. "Now the only other possibility, and like everything else," he said, dropping the volume of his voice. "You didn't hear it from me, is that it was a hit—some kind of retaliation for something or other. The thing is the guy picking up Adella that night was Giovanni Fandano's kid."

"No fooling, Frank D'Angelo!"

"You knew! You know, I'm never sure if you're 'that good' or just 'bullshit lucky'. Anyway, if you were Satan himself, to save my soul I couldn't tell you any more. That's all I have, Mickey."

"You know, after listening to those feeble alternatives, even I'm beginning to think I did it." He grinned. "Given that list, *hell*, I'm convinced *I'm* their best suspect, but don't quote me on it. Apparently, it's an easy sale this week and there are just too many buyers at the moment."

"Here, let me run the plates and see what we come up with," said Garrett, logging onto the DMV site. "See, that's what I was afraid of."

"What?"

"Well look, this could take a while. You did say local plates?"

"I didn't, no, but that's right, they were. Late model, red Grand Prix," Lannigan repeated, watching the numbers on the screen scrolling by faster than he could read them.

"Okay, well you were right, it's definitely a rental. Do you walk around with a horseshoe up your ass? Year, let's say two thousand two and see what happens?

Bingo! There it is. There's your car, buddy boy. It was leased from the 'AAA' Car Rental Agency in Delray. They're located on Lexington Boulevard about five blocks from here. You must live under a friggin' lucky star, my friend."

"Thanks, Jim, that makes us just about even," he said slapping his friend on the back of the shoulder.

"Poker Saturday night?"

"Right, Saturday night," he muttered, noting the timeline. "Yeah," he replied sounding preoccupied. "Same place, Julio's?"

"No, I spoke with your friend, Skully, like you suggested. He thinks it's a great idea, so we're downstairs in the back of the Mayflower. The Dungeon Room, he calls it. He even hired a couple of frilly, blonde wenches to distract you like I asked."

"Well, just tell him to have Napoleon close by and chilled for a change. Oh, and whatever you do, don't forget those prints, Jimbo, thanks," he added, opening the door into the hall.

"By the way," said Garrett, glancing down at his watch. Then, looking over his shoulder at the detective, half in and half out, he hoisted his wrist with a Cardinal timepiece on it for Mick to see. "As for the time of day, it's four forty-two." He laughed, logging off and hearing the door close behind him...

Chapter 20

As we race the winding highway in a mad dash for its end, we'll often hit a hurdle having somehow missed the bend. That's when the driver changes gears and slowing down, gains far more ground, just by switching lanes and weaving through the traffic out of town…

—4.51 p.m. —

Lannigan pulled up in front of the AAA Car Rental Agency on Lexington Boulevard. There wasn't a soul around, but inside, past a large, picture window, was a woman, a tall brunette mulling about behind a counter.

The detective walked in, smiled and went over to where she was standing.

"Hi there," he said.

"Hi yourself," she replied, returning his smile. "And wait, don't tell me; you're here to rent a car?"

"You'd think so, wouldn't yah?" Mick paused, distracted momentarily by the highlights in her hair. "In fact, I'm a police officer looking for someone who did," he replied. "You're not here alone, that can't be safe this time of day?"

"Cameras," remarked the young agent, pointing to the ceiling behind her up in the corner.

"Corruption," suggested Lannigan, smiling, pointing at the window towards Lexington and the heart of the downtown core with his thumb.

"A girlfriend will be along in about ten minutes with my ride, but thanks for your concern," she said, along with another captivating smile.

"I should've known you were a bright girl; brunettes usually are. So that camera tapes the coming and goings, and it's always on?"

"Always, and it's hooked into a security system. It was Ms. Crenshaw's idea, the owner, and a darn good one. You won't be surprised to discover she's also a brunette," declared the woman, turning to face the camera and grinning as she waved at it. Then, gazing back at the detective, she gently stroked her bangs away from her eyes. "So what is it that I can do for you, Officer?"

"It's Lannigan, ma'am, Lieutenant Lannigan," he told her, not even bothering to show any identification. "We had a tip that someone we're very anxious to get our hands on, was seen driving a late model, red Grand Prix. One of yours it seems based on a partial plate we got." He hesitated, giving up a covert glance to the camera. "Anyway, that's why *I'm* here. It might be nothing, but we have to check every little, weak and weary possibility. You just never know, right, Chief?"

he submitted, smiling up into the lens and appealing to her lighter side.

She laughed. "I can certainly take a look for you. What's his name, Lieutenant?" asked the brunette, reaching for a clipboard hanging on the wall behind her.

"Well, earlier today it was Vincent Demilo, a large man with dark hair and a mustache if it helps."

"Right, I think I know who you mean, yeah, with a scar on his cheek," she added, stroking hers with a finger to mark the location for the officer. "He was in this morning, just after I opened as a matter of fact," she told him, flipping through several of the pages clamped to the clipboard. "Yeah, here it is. According to this, his name is still Demilo. The truth is, he insisted on the Grand Prix and as you said, it was definitely that middle-aged preference, fire engine red."

"You didn't happen to notice how he arrived, you know, by himself or with someone?"

"Sure, I was unlocking the door when I heard a taxi pull up in the parking lot behind me. Conley Cabs since I know you guys *love* details, and the man you described, scar and all, got out and pointed out the Pontiac to me. And except for the cabby, he was alone."

"You have an answer for everything. At this rate, I'll be out of your gorgeous, brunette hair in no time," he said, charming the woman with a dose of silvery-tongued flattery.

"Then I guess I'll just have to slow down, won't I?" she whispered, finding his lips with her eyes.

Lannigan grinned. "So tell me then, and please… take your time. Does that all-knowing sheet also tell you what address the man used?"

"Absolutely," she smiled, taking his advice, "819 Delaware apartment 412 over in Conley, which also explains his choice of taxi."

"Yes, it does, but for how long?"

"You've stumped me, Mr. Lanni…" She faltered. "That is to say, Lieutenant. I don't know that one I'm afraid. It just says he lives there," she replied. "Ordinarily, that's not one of our questions."

"No." He chuckled. "Sorry, no, I meant how long did he take the car for, miss?"

"Candi, it's Candi."

"Now isn't that different, Candi," Mick repeated. "Short *and* sweet." He grinned.

"Yes, that's it exactly, different. I'm aspiring to be an actress one day. It may take a while, but in the meantime, I have this job. My stage name is Candi Kane but with a 'K' on Kane, get it? So what do you think?"

"Hohoho," he replied smiling. "I think you should do well around Christmas, especially if you can locate this fellow, Kringle, I keep hearing so much about." He winked. "Now did you say when this guy would be returning the car?"

"Oh right, the car," she remarked, staring at the colour of his eyes and then redirecting hers, reading through the form as she followed her finger down the page. "Yeah, it says he took our special: three days with

216

a midsize or better and the fourth is half price, including unlimited mileage. So that would make it the eleventh, next Monday around ten a.m."

"Damn! That's too late!" he muttered, tapping the bottom of his fist on the edge of the counter.

"What's too late?"

"Monday," replied the detective. Tomorrow, later this evening, five minutes ago, he mused. The bastard will be out of the city, and most likely the country by then. "Look, between you, me and that clipboard you're holding, he's a desperate man, miss, so watch yourself if he does decide to come back. Yeah, I know, the camera," he acknowledged seeing her point towards it. "Still, he's extremely violent, unpredictable and wanted in connection with a string of homicides. And sometimes the pictures those contraptions take aren't very pretty in the end." Lannigan hesitated. "Anyway, just don't be here alone when, and if, the time comes, and thanks for the information," he said getting ready to leave.

"*Murder*," she voiced. "That's a whole 'nother kettle of fish. Perhaps this is my lucky day you wandering in, and yours too, me being here."

"Right… that's what today is, Miss Kane, my *lucky* day." He sniggered, willing to embrace her choice of phrase and the hook dangling in front of him with the bait he recognized all too well. "Yeah, okay, I'll bite, how exactly is it my lucky day?"

"Well with all the thefts and fraud lately, people using false IDs and stolen charge cards, not to mention insurance rates skyrocketing, the company has started placing small transmitters inside the dash of our vehicles so we can track the ones that mysteriously disappear off the face of the earth. The reduction on our insurance almost pays for the inconvenience. And we've heard, by way of the distributor, that even some taxicab companies are taking advantage of the technology."

"Don't tell me, Ms. Crenshaw," he suggested.

"Say, that's right! It must be that dark hair of yours," she kidded. "If you'd like, I can take a look on our 'IT', excuse me, our Integrated Tracking system?"

"No shi—"

"Yeah, no shi—" she said, imitating him exactly, and grinning. "I figure if you're able to do your job, it'll make mine a bit easier come Monday morning," she confessed.

"You're saying you can tell me where the man is, or his car anyway?"

"Precisely," said the rental agent, slipping into a back office with her clipboard in hand. "It shouldn't take long, not that I'm trying to get rid of you or anything."

Sitting down at the company's tracking screen, punching in the code, the licence plate of the car in question, 'XDL-0349', she'd soon activated the sensor and located the vehicle's whereabouts. After only a few minutes, she returned. Lannigan was still hugging the counter and tapping his fingers impatiently while he stared off into space.

"The C-IT system says the car is sitting in the vicinity of the airport in Conley, Lieutenant Lannigan. And it's not running, according to the motion detector."

"That's *absolutely* amazing. I've never heard of anything like it. It's brilliant! How far away does the signal reach?"

"Just like our mileage policy, it's unlimited as well." She beamed. "The Nortel representative from Canada guarantees you can trace it to 'anywhere on, or off, the face of the planet'."

The airport, he mused—just like I figured, scared shitless. Sure, the son-of-a-bitch read the letter, discovered who was after D'Angelo's killer and panicked. Demilo, or whoever he is, is flying the coop. Back to Missouri maybe, he thought, suddenly motivated to ask Cassandra Carlisle about a particular address in Kansas City. "Interesting, thanks, Candi, Miss Kane. I really do owe you, big time."

"I don't need 'big time', Lieutenant, just a good time," she sighed. "Anytime," she added, gathering a smile and watching him turn up the collar of his coat while, at the same time, turning down her tempting offer for the moment.

"Thanks again," he replied, noticing that it was nearly dusk and seeing several streetlights come on up and down the boulevard.

"You're welcome, Lieutenant."

"Yeah, listen, about that; unfortunately, I'm sort of involved right now. Though, if that situation was to take a sudden turn, which is quite often the case, certainly in my life anyway, I do have your number," he said, and opening the door, stopped to look back at the tall, slender knockout once more. He was easily willing to contemplate a change of heart if he wasn't so preoccupied with the rest of his life; all at once considering how Adella Hughes had decided to up and call it quits out-of-the-blue, one day. Then how his secretary had reacted to his latest female client for no apparent reason holed up in his apartment. How his new, blonde lady friend, Cassandra Carlisle, was all over the map with him from the get-go, and then all over him, he mused, and needing a score card to keep up. "If it should come to pass that we do get together, maybe you could explain to me what it is about women that causes them to be so emotional all the time. It definitely makes the ride more complicated. Like a roller coaster, sure, with fringe benefits, but a bumpy ride just the same," he admitted, setting her straight and smiling as he left.

Descending the half-dozen steps to the parking lot, the detective hurried to the silver sedan. As he slipped in behind the wheel, for the first time since being snatched from his bed at gunpoint, Mick Lannigan reasoned out his next move and headed for home…

Part VI

Chapter 21

Dire, dark and frigid is how he found the second floor. While his flat was calm, but compromised without a window and a door. Inside looking for a message like a dog might for a bone. Oh yes, looking for so many things, but most of all, the telephone…

—6.12 p.m.—

The apartment was in a cocoon of darkness by the time Mick arrived back. Even the outer hall was chilled while a breeze made its way effortlessly through the broken window leading from the fire escape. As he entered the flat, there was a subtle scent of aftershave still in the air. He knew it wasn't his. Aqua-Velva, he noted, remembering Skully's comment as the same aroma wafted across the bar one night down at the Mayflower.

Quickly removing the .45 from under his coat and turning on the lights after feeling around for the wall switch, Lannigan immediately realized the place was a shambles and that whoever did it was long gone. The door was lying across the carpet again after Doris's desk had been upended and wedged into the couch.

Convinced it was looters, he began assessing the damage while, at the same time, combing the debris for his phone.

Instead though, he was sidetracked, spotting a black mug hugging the corner of a baseboard in the hallway. He picked it up, blew out the dust and an unlucky spider seeking shelter from the cold and, getting an idea, set it down on top of one of the highboys. Rifling through the drawers, Mick eventually came across what he was looking for, a bottle of bourbon he kept handy for emergencies and just such an occasion. 'Just in case' he needed to quiet his nerves a little or chase away the chill on a bitter night. Taking no more than a brief look around at a candid cross-section of his life, and much of it in ruins, 'just in case' suddenly presented itself, he decided, in living colour. Front and centre, and rising like a phoenix from the ashes, standing at his doorstep and knocking on the very door that he found himself standing on as well.

From what he could tell, the only thing untouched was his souvenir Louisville slugger leaning up against the wall in the corner, ironically waiting to deal with any intruders who might drop by unexpectedly or unannounced. With that thought, and refusing to relinquish his silent partner for the time being, the detective reached over and righted the desk, all at once seeing the base of the phone and its receiver still attached, five feet away at the end of the coiled, black cable. Picking up the pieces, he set his secretary's telephone on the desktop as the unit jingled its displeasure at being manhandled.

Standing there taking a long, slow drink, Lannigan noticed a light begin to blink on the panel. Quickly grabbing the toppled chair-on-wheels and flipping it right side up, he sat down with his eyes glued to the entrance, his bourbon in hand and his ivory handled Colt .45 placed conveniently alongside the phone, also at his fingertips.

Dialling his service and then his password, he leaned back, took another drink and, making his selection, waited for the first of two messages to play out. It was from Jim Garrett.

"Listen, Mickey, I thought I should call and let you know as soon as possible. You did say it was serious and it's not like you to mince words. That matchbook of yours told me quite a story, but then like most good mysteries, it left me hanging for the ending I think you wanted. There were, literally, a handful of prints as you can imagine, but there just weren't enough quality ridges to do anything with, I'm afraid. They were either smudged or non-existent in many cases. I used so much fluorescent powder on it that, well, I'll be glowing in the dark for *about* a week." He laughed. "Anyway, besides your Neanderthal-type thumb all over the cover, we found Brian Bettman's prints as well. He's clean as a whistle, not so much as a parking violation. But there was also a third fingerprint. Unfortunately, the best I could get was a partial eight-point that will take far longer to match up, if it's even possible at all—sorry, Mick. Still, with the high frequency of loops in the pattern I was able to lift, I'm taking an educated guess that the fellow is European. You're just going to have to learn to keep your grubby, great paws off the evidence, my friend," he said. "As for the book, we found two perfect sets, textbook imprints you might say. One I couldn't identify and the other, a male by the name of Ricciardi. First name, Lonzo," Jim said, pausing suddenly as if someone had interrupted him. Mick could detect the sound of faraway voices in the background while his friend covered the mouthpiece.

"That name seems very familiar," mumbled the detective, finishing off his bourbon and waiting eagerly to hear the rest of the playback.

"Now, where was I?" said Garrett. "Oh yeah, the prints. I have to assume you snatched the book from the same place you emailed me from since you mentioned his name in the subject line. Anyway, making the connection, I knew you'd want me to run a trace on him, after all, I don't have a life, right?"

Mick grinned. "Of course, Lonzo *Ricciardi, right*," he muttered, sloppily pouring himself another finger or two of bourbon and smiling as he set the bottle back down.

"I checked the book on this guy, here goes. Have a seat, though if I know you, you're already sitting down with a glass of Napoleon in your hand, no doubt." Close enough, thought Mick, hoisting the Planet Hollywood mug to his lips for a return engagement. "Lonzo Ricciardi: One five-year term for insurance fraud in eighty-seven. No outstanding warrants, *at the moment,* however it's only a matter of time. He's got a record as long as your monkey, Mick, everything from assault, armed robbery, two counts of B and E to attempted murder, not to mention his fondness for fraud. He also appears to match up with some unidentified, and incomplete, prints at another crime scene we have in our databanks—that, I'm still looking into so thanks for the business. Charming fellow indeed, but here's the other thing. The man's got enough aliases to field a fuckin' basketball team, Mick. Going by such favourites as Louis Malagio to Joe Righetti, Antelo Pilattzi…"

"Son-of-a-bitch!" said Mick, unconsciously leaning closer to the phone and hanging onto every word Jim Garrett had to say.

"… I hope I pronounced that last one right… and…"

"Vincent Demilo," remarked Lannigan, jumping in.

"Vincent Demilo, somebody Sabatini and as you can well imagine, the list goes on and sadly, on and on. Fortunately, I spilled coffee on the rest. So there you go, tough guy. I hope some of this stuff helps you. I know it's going to keep me occupied for weeks to come, oh and did I say thanks," said Garrett in a slightly sarcastic tone.

"Haha, *oh it helps*, Jimbo, you bet my ass it does," he said, slamming the desk with the flat of his hand and then grabbing his mug, taking a good, stiff drink to celebrate. "Thanks, buddy," Mick whispered, staring back at the phone.

"A piece of advice though, he strikes me as a nasty bit of work, so keep your eye on this one if you *do* run into him."

I think it's too late, Mick noted. I think he already ran into me. *Hell*, maybe things really do happen for a reason and it was opportunity knocking after all, he mused, calling up the other message.

"Yeah, it's Jim again. I got distracted by another friend of yours, anyway, an addendum you lucky Irish *bastard*. A couple of things really, first Stern was just in here. It seems a fellow by the name of Brian Bettman turned up dead at the Plaza this afternoon. I don't suppose you'd know anything about that? Nah, I didn't think so. Probably just one of those rare coincidences neither one of us believe in, huh? But that's not exactly why I called either. Inside that book you left with me, I found something you might find rather interesting. I know I did! Wedged between pages one four two and one four three—and I have no idea how significant the page numbers are—I discovered a piece of a document, quite possibly a marriage licence, dated August third, 1999 and the word, 'Kansas'. But that's not the best part. Imagine my surprise when I dusted it and found pinch prints, simply meaning they were put there with some amount of force, and determined that they belonged to… hold onto your hat, Mickey. Are you holding on to something, because this is huge, buddy… Adella Hughes, of all people," he announced with some spirit and a great deal of pride.

"*What*!" exclaimed Lannigan, sitting up straight in his seat!

"Who owes who *now*? It blew me away. And that's not a probable or a close match, it's a dead-ringer," he announced impulsively, though followed by an awkward and weighty moment of silence. "Sorry, Mick, poor choice of words, but you must be onto something. Anyway, that's it from this end. Later," he said, hanging up.

Saving the second message as well, and convinced he knew where Demilo was likely headed, the detective dialled the airport to book a flight for Kansas City. Then he called Doris Harrington's apartment and asked to speak with Cassandra Carlisle.

"Hi, gorgeous, how's Doris treating you? She sounds upset again?"

"Fine, sweetie, what's up? Have you located my husband?"

"Not yet, but I think I'm making some progress. Do you know the name Ricciardi off hand?"

"No," she admitted immediately. Mick believed her.

"How about Demilo, Vincent Demilo, does that do anything for you?"

"I've never heard it before. Why so many questions and who are all these people?" she asked, anxious and waiting for his response.

"Well, for now they're just characters in a book," he replied.

"What do you mean, Mick?"

"They're acquaintances of your husband's. That's all you really have to know."

"What's going on? Why won't you tell me anything?"

"Because there's nothing to tell, good-looking." He paused. "I have one last question. I need your address in Kansas City."

"Why," she replied.

"Why? Because I'm on the trail of that dragon you wanted me to slay and I think I finally know where he's headed, so just relax. You're safe for the time being and nothing's going to happen to you if you stay put like I tell you, got it?"

"Got it," she said in a soft voice, somehow reassured while she rhymed off what he wanted to know.

"Good, now just sit tight until you hear from me, and, well… if you don't hear anything by say, the day after tomorrow, expect a very long-distance call sometime." He grinned.

"What? Are you leaving tonight, and what about Bri—"

"Gotta go, gorgeous," he said, and hung up before she could finish.

Following the phone call, Mick sat back and stared at his gun suddenly hearing the elevator doors open. Then, pouring a bourbon chaser, he calmly reached for the weapon, raised it deliberately and, pointing the barrel towards the entrance, watched Snake appear as big as life in the doorway.

"Where's your shadow? Oh that's right, you can't see it at night." He smiled, gently putting the gun back down before downing his drink anyway. "I'd ask you to join me but, as you can see, I don't have another mug; then again, maybe your hands are clean. What do you say?" he asked, ready to pour.

"Funny guy; apparently you're running out of furniture as fast as you're running out of time." Snake grinned. "But it must be gratifying to know you've inadvertently managed to combine junkyard elegance with audacious whimsy, and all without leaving the comfort of your home."

"Let's only hope you run out of clumsy, clever lines just as quickly. And on the subject of belongings and where some of us belong, it seems that every time I find my place like, *this*," said Mick, waving his arms to reintroduce the clutter, "you're just around the corner. Isn't that interesting, *and* disturbing, all in the same breath—a coincidence perhaps? I don't know. Still, it could certainly get a man to thinking."

"But you don't believe in coincidence, Sherlock. Remember?"

"Well, for *you*, I'm tempted to make an exception. So what brings you out of hiding, and how did you know I'd even be here? Or maybe that wasn't an issue when you slithered in?" suggested Lannigan, sounding somewhat perturbed by, and suspicious of, his unexpected presence.

"Don't forget you're my responsibility, Lannigan, for the next little while at least. I promised I'd be in your neighbourhood, and I never break a promise. Besides, I wouldn't want anything to happen to you now, would I? I'm only doing what Fandano wants me to, and that's making sure the goods don't get spoiled, if you get me, and I'm quite sure you do," he gibed.

"Yeah, right," said Lannigan, hesitating, confused somewhat by Snake's sudden candour. "Well, as even you can tell from all the way over there, I'm just fine no thanks to you, but thanks for stopping by and, bu-bye," said Mick, dismissing him with a backhanded wave. When Snake didn't take the hint, Lannigan spoke up. "Was there something else you'd like?" asked the detective, feeling the liquor take the bite off a long day and the hour begin to sting a little less.

"It doesn't appear like you're having an awful lot of luck, Lannigan?"

"Luck is it?" he replied and all at once getting the distinct impression that the man was fishing. "Well, neither did I think so at first, but you know what? Things change, Snake. Yes, they do, and in ways you could never imagine. I know I couldn't," he said. "Still, I'm amazed. I didn't think snakes could fish. What's your game, sidewinder? I can usually read between the lines, but they seem a little blurry right now. I'm not sure if that's your writing technique, the liquor or the way I'm sitting, haha, haha!"

"Time's running out, so drink up, funny boy. Why *not* enjoy your last twenty-four hours on earth, right?" he remarked.

"Twenty-four," replied Mick, getting louder, glancing at the clock on the wall, smiling and all at once aware that there were two things in the apartment unscathed. "First of all, about the time, you're wrong. Secondly, you're way off base about me and 'C', didn't anybody ever tell you that when you're tailing someone, you're not supposed to actually let them see you?" He laughed. "Now get the hell out of here and go find your shadow, even if it takes all night," he insisted, suddenly getting up and walking past his own shadow towards the back of the flat.

Turning up the thermostat, Mick Lannigan retreated to his bedroom and closed the door. He tossed his trench coat over a chair and, sitting on the edge of the bed, setting his alarm, the detective contemplated a paradox of a personal nature. He knew he didn't trust the man standing in his living room, not as far as he could throw him if that was even possible, which is why he was still standing out there in his living room, he mused. And yet, he also knew that Snake would never kill him either, yet. Stretching out on the rumpled bed, adjusting his fedora over his eyes, Lannigan fell asleep almost before his head hit the pillow.

Snake on the other hand—christened Paul Tagliano—never did leave. The man with the hairy knuckles had other ideas. With his shadow sitting outside, the man inside made himself at home on the sofa with his faithful .357 magnum draped across his chest, and waited...

Chapter 22

People come and people go, each with purpose and or rhyme. But all come for a reason or a season, or perhaps forever, given time. And if that adage holds its truth, well then how fortunate are we. To be destined ships passing in the night, on this remote and sleepless sea...

—THURSDAY, MAY 7th—3.02 a.m.—

Hearing the alarm and sitting up slowly, even awkwardly, it took a moment or two for Lannigan to figure out where he was. Staring at the mirror and suddenly remembering his situation, the detective grabbed his hat from the floor, his coat off the back of a chair and flew out of the apartment like he, or it, was under siege. He was on his way to the airport in Conley—better than forty-five minutes away if he could even catch a decent wave of lights—where he'd grab a red-eye to Kansas City, scheduled to depart at four fifty a.m.

As the detective raced the interstate, challenging the traffic, his muddled thoughts and the speed limit, he returned to a conversation he'd had with Cassie shortly after taking the last straightaway headed for the 'Daily Double', the one and only night they were together and playing another kind of gambit.

"So you believe attractive women, blondes specifically, are your downfall," she whispered, teasing his ear with her tongue.

"Maybe I do," he shuddered, attempting to deny her delicate caress and effective advances. "I give you exhibit 'A' your honour," he said, holding her by the upper arms as she screamed with delight, giggling. "But I just can't walk away from the well," Mick admitted, lying back, putting his hands behind his head and staring at the ceiling.

"Well, you might want to consider taking a page from an American institution," she suggested, smiling down at him from her knees while he contemplated kneading her firm, white breasts.

"What?" he asked, his mind wandering and vacillating at the comment.

"Abbott and Costello!" she began. "'That's okay', says Costello after losing another girl to the dashing singer in Act II. 'I'd just as soon marry a homely girl anyway'. 'A homely girl could leave you just the same', replied Abbott. 'Yeah, but who cares', said Lou," she recounted, tumbling down next to him.

"I get it, but no, I don't think so, darlin'. I'm a risk-taker. I've always been a risk-taker. And I'll always be one. I've never believed in taking the easy way," he confessed. "And somehow, I end up paying for that way of thinking every time, but no. It's not in the cards, little lady. You'll do just fine, I'm afraid," he said with a smile looking over at her. "Good night, gorgeous, or should I say good morning," said Mick, noting the time, rolling onto his side and turning off the light.

As the blonde crawled across his body, nearly straddling the man only to kiss him in the dark, her warm, writhing thighs rubbing against his, he had a sudden urge to gamble away his good-standing on a trifecta and, putting it all on the line, go for the gate. Go to the well one more time he mused, making use of his own analogy. And just like the clubhouse chute, it was the precise instant his luck turned too, the exact moment Lannigan realized his undeniable fate, and surprisingly, it was nothing what he expected. Sometimes it pays to go out on a limb, thought the detective, fondling her charms while she bit his lip, leaning into him. After all he determined, manhandling the woman and swallowing her tongue in a heightened upheaval of lust, that's where the fruit is if you don't happen to fall, and the longer the limb and the tougher the climb, the sweeter the fruit at the end of it all…

Chapter 23

I'm not an ardent disciple of the 'Good Book', however, until somebody has the balls to subsume its more insightful scriptures into the justice system— as God intended—we're all going to bear the burden for a long, long time to come. 'An eye for an eye,' it makes a great deal of sense to the church, evidently. And aren't these students of the sacred writ eloquent to the extreme when it comes to such things as morality? From muggings to manslaughter, apply the law and you *will* get your order. 'What say you, my group of twelve? How do you find this defendant?' 'Guilty my lord,' replied the foreman'. 'The ayes have it then. Will the judged please rise and face his accusers. Based on the verdict from this assembly of your peers in the matter, and murder, of Brian Bettman, I sentence you on behalf of the laws of heaven and earth, the quick *and* the dead. I commit you, he who is charged with pulling the trigger and ending another's life, to the same fate, three bullets in your throat by a court appointed executioner, and may God have mercy on all our souls...'

As daylight touched down on the state of Missouri, so did the wheels of the 767, screeching across the endless, black tarmac. Lannigan gathered his one piece of carry-on and then sat back down, all at once reminded of his shadow, seeing the sun enter the cabin of the plane. He wondered which tree, rock or door he would be hiding behind while they taxied up the runway.

Within the hour, the out-of-towner was leaving the terminal and waving down a cab as another pulled up beside him in its place. Standing at the curb, he watched the tinted rear window begin to roll down slowly.

"You look like you could use a ride," suggested the well-dressed bodyguard in his usual domineering tone.

"A ride, is it? I'm already on the ride of my life. The best you could offer is a footnote, and isn't this a little outside your jurisdiction?" replied Mick, bending over, shading his eyes and eventually gazing at the man's shadow on the far side in the back seat as well.

"Until midnight, you are my jurisdiction, Sherlock, get in," demanded the man in no uncertain terms from his seat by the window.

"Well, since you put it so nicely, why not?" he said, getting in the front seat.

"Where to," asked the taxi driver in a strong, Middle-East accent.

"Five hundred and nineteen west, 47th Street," replied Lannigan.

Twenty minutes later, the cabby pulled up to Demilo's apartment building with the three men inside, all having very little to say while the long-winded and difficult-to-understand driver entertained them with his knowledge of the city until Snake bluntly told him to, '*Shut the fuck up and just drive!*'

"How did you find out about this place?" asked Snake while the car rolled to a stop at the entrance, covered by a lengthy awning and running from the curbside of the cab to the double glass doors.

"His wife," replied Mick, as Snake stepped out from the taxi first, his body language indicating he was uneasy and even circumspect with the detective's discovery.

"How's that possible? Ricciardi's wife is dead," sighed the Snake, soft and sluggish.

"Yes, in fact, several of them are." He glowered, having to concede the reality. "But his present one, *isn't*," offered the detective, suddenly finding it more than curious the man knew it was Ricciardi's residence to begin with, but on top of that, that at least one of his wives was dead. Gaining little by stirring the pot, Lannigan elected to leave the issue—a slip of the tongue perhaps—alone for the time being. Besides, the venue wasn't to his liking and a better opportunity would surely present itself, even if it were as his own 'slip of the tongue' for Fandano's benefit.

"Stay here," Snake ordered to his silent sidekick while harbouring a look on his face that Lannigan couldn't quite discern. "This won't take long."

Once the two men were out, Snake slammed the door of the cab and together they swaggered toward the lobby past a doorman.

"Good morning, gentlemen," said the uniformed attendant, smiling as the pair swept by him.

"Thanks, bud," remarked the detective, entering first.

He checked the listing inside a glass case mounted to the floor like a preacher's pulpit; the nameplate next to suite 104 confirmed the apartment belonged to Mr. and Mrs. Antelo Pilattzi.

Before even reaching 104, Mick Lannigan pulled out the key chain he'd found in Bettman's hotel suite.

"You even have a *key*," commented the Italian, breathing down the detective's neck.

"Like I said, I know his wife... intimately. You met her the other day," he said, grinning. "And maybe it's just my imagination, but I get the distinct impression you're taking all this a little *too* personal, sidewinder?"

"You're right," Tagliano faltered momentarily, hearing the tumbler click and the deadbolt release. "It is your imagination. And let's not forget that you're the one staring down the last day of the rest of his life, not me. Enjoy it while you can, snoop," he added almost as if to taunt, a timely reminder to distract the private eye from his purpose for being there. "So take your time," said Snake, watching Lannigan carefully open the door.

"Still, between the two of us, I'd have to say you're the anxious one. Odd when you consider that it's my life on the line; yes, it is curious, indeed. Curiouser and curiouser," he suggested, hesitating, seeing the impressive layout of the apartment. "Now why do you suppose that is?"

"Let it go, Lannigan. You're talking through that hat of yours. I don't know what you *think* you're onto, but you're dead wrong. Other than a case of desperation, you got nothin'," asserted the pug. "And what do you hope to find anyway?"

"I guess if I've got nothing, according to you anyway, I should settle for just about anything at all. But more to the point I sense, what is it you hope I *don't* find?" he asked him right back while perusing the suite.

There wasn't a pillow out of place. It was neat and orderly bordering on the obsessive, the model room for a would-be buyer looking at a setting out of a Disney, feel-good movie.

"That's ridiculous. That hit on the head yesterday morning must've knocked more than a few screws loose. I think it knocked you loopy!"

"Or maybe it just knocked some sense into me," Mick replied, bound for the bedroom. Enticed by the thought of getting a glimpse into Cassie's life at the same time and beyond a subtle cue that might guide him down the right path, he wasn't entirely sure what he was after.

The spacious back room was just the opposite of the rest of the apartment, beginning with clothes strewn over the floor that started near a walk-in closet. There were half-open drawers in a mirrored bureau with more clothing draped over them. On an armoire in the corner, he spotted a picture of Cassandra Carlisle with her husband and, picking it up to examine more closely, noticed an empty jewellery box with one of its back hinges snapped off in the middle of the bed. After a hasty inspection of the walk-in, the detective returned to witness Snake enjoying the view from the balcony.

"*Well*," inquired Snake. "Are you just about done here?"

"Tell me something, when we pulled up outside, you knew exactly where we were, and why, I have to assume. As if you'd been here before, now how's that possible, I wonder?" he asked, checking the hall closet. It's a small world, but suddenly there was more than just the one, and some of them are starting to collide he considered, rummaging through the pockets of a suede coat hanging by itself.

Snake wandered back in from the balcony. "His name came up, Ricciardi's, shortly after the explosion. I did a bit of my own snooping on Fandano's behalf. Points are points when you're near the top, and sometimes the difference between that brass ring you keep reaching for and a piece of lead you spend your life avoiding."

"Well that's all well and good, but the name downstairs, it's Pilattzi."

"When his name came up, it came up a couple of times and a couple of ways," Snake said with a deadpan expression. "So I came down here to see the man, a skunk by any name still stinks, and discovered not only he wasn't bright enough to pull it off, the explosion I mean, but that he had an ironclad alibi at the same time."

"*Really*, ironclad is it? I didn't realize there *was* such a beast. You're certainly forgiving when it's convenient, I must say. So you think this is a wild goose chase then? Well, you know what?" said Lannigan changing his tone dramatically, "I think you're full of shit! Though, I suppose it would explain how you knew about his wife."

"Exactly," he replied, watching Lannigan pick up a pad next to the phone.

"Let's just test those sleuth-like qualities of yours, see if you can scare up a pencil, Mr. Investigator. Check that drawer in the desk," suggested Mick. "Never mind," he added, before Snake could even change his direction. "I found one." A golfer, he thought, grabbing the stubby just above its sharpened tip. "A little trick my father showed me," he remarked, rubbing the lead of the pencil lightly over the near invisible imprint on the pad of paper. "First time I've ever tried it. Sure hope it works," he said, smiling and obviously pleased with the results. "Well there we have it," concluded the detective, flipping the pencil on the table and tearing the top sheet off. "Hmmm, a phone number perhaps," he declared, dialling the seven-digit sequence.

"Hello ... I'm sorry, you're very quick. Who did you say you were again...? Universal Travel," he repeated. "No kidding, I do have the right number then. So you arrange bookings, flights, that kind of thing...? Great, well this is Lieutenant Lannigan from the KCPD and, as it happens, I'm calling from an active crime scene. Ordinarily I wouldn't be using this phone. However, I'm interested in knowing if someone else has called you recently from this number."

"It would be difficult to tell, Lieutenant. Unfortunately, being a small local outlet like we are, we don't have such luxuries as call display, an answering machine or even a file clerk. It's pretty much me here by myself most days, and if I don't get the phone, we don't get the business."

"I see, well then could you tell me if anyone contacted you under the name of Demilo in the last little while?"

"No, no one by that name," she said.

"How about Pilattzi then, Antelo Pilattzi?"

"Not that either, I think I'd remember. Perhaps it was another agency, Lieutenant?"

"I don't believe so, miss, no, Ricciardi, does that sound familiar at all?" he went on, tossing her one more name and wishing he could recall the others from the list Garrett had mentioned.

"Why, yes it does. He called here around closing time yesterday, a very high-strung gentleman to be sure. Hang on, I'll check the records," she offered, setting the phone down. "Yes, Mr. Ricciardi purchased a ticket to Cancún, one way as a matter of fact. Well, it is the perfect place any time of year," she remarked.

"I'll take your word for it. Still, I have a feeling even Cancún isn't perfect enough for this guy, but thank you," said Lannigan, quickly hanging up and grinning at the man watching him from across the room with a strained facial cast. "Hell, if my luck holds out a little longer, I'll be free, clear and on my way by dinnertime," he announced, tucking the phone number in his shirt pocket while he made his way to the door...

Chapter 24

**What you see is what you get is what you often hear.
But what you see even when you do isn't always very
clear. And what you know is all you have when all
you see is true. So if what you have is second hand,
is that enough to see you through?**

—9.47 a.m.—

Arriving back at the terminal, both Mick Lannigan and
his escort, Paul Tagliano, had their own ideas as to
where they were headed.

"Whoa! *Whoa, whoa*! Just where do you think
you're off to, Sherlock?" inquired Snake, grabbing the
detective by the ball of the shoulder as he hurried his
pace towards the international flights counter.

"What are you talking about?" Mick replied,
turning around. "You heard my conversation with the
travel agent, Cancún, the Yucatan Peninsula. That's
where Demilo is and I plan to bring him back, with or
without you. Preferably without, and if possible before
midnight, so I don't have time to waste arguing!"

"Nah, uh-uh, smart-ass, I don't think so. It's too pat
somehow. It sounds like a ruse to me. I think this is far

more than bounty hunting, and you can't run far enough, Lannigan. I won't let you," he said. "It's *my* life if I do."

"Don't be ridiculous, a ruse," he snorted. "But you're fucking right! This is way more than tracking down Fandano's ticket to a clear conscience. It's about saving my goddamn life! Why would I take a fade when I'm so close now? I know exactly who murdered his son. I've got his killer dead to rights. Enough evidence to hang three or four of him, and being right keeps me from being dead. Now I just have to find the son-of-a-bitch and bring him back before he changes his name again," Mick declared, stumbling, desperately flipping through the man's scenario and looking for the precise page Snake was on. "If your boss wants this guy as bad as I know he does, I'll need to take a little detour to the island. And according to the light-show on that board up there, the next, *and last*, flight out till tomorrow leaves in less than an hour, and with security the way it is, I'll be lucky to make it at all."

"You don't know how lucky." Snake laughed, caring little for the man's argument or his situation and, all at once, even for the man himself. "Let's just do the math, fly-boy. It's *my* ass if you're not back this side of midnight and, believe it or not, you're just not worth my ass. And the numbers don't appear to be in your favour. I figure," he said, staring at the Rolex strapped to the underside of his wrist and struggling with the calculations in his head, "less than fourteen hours. Now it's at least a four-hour flight one way and, from there, more than seven back to Conley, not including airport security at both fuckin' ends. That leaves what?"

"A good couple of hours maybe," declared the detective to save time, "on a decent day and I don't have many of either."

"Well, there's your answer then," replied Snake, grinning like a wild-eyed hyena.

"Look," said Mick, experiencing a late wakeup call in the way of an unexpected blow to the head as well as his chances, and hushed for an instant, evidently derailed and promptly rerouted by the brick wall he was suddenly running into. "You can believe me when I tell you I *will* get the bastard and deliver him to Fandano, *and* in time. You and your boss have my word on that."

"*Your* word, so let me get this straight, with your life on the line, I've got *your* word, haha," he said, glancing at his partner. "*Haha*... no dice, Lannigan, not going to happen in my lifetime, or yours either apparently. Your *word* is worth even less than your life right about now; no, we're all three of us, going back. And as I pointed out, between your sorry ass and mine, you don't have a hope in hell, hotshot, which is just about where you're headed. Giovanni said by midnight or your ass is his. I was there, it is."

"All right, then why don't *you* go find him? Gain a batch of those brownie points you seem to be chasing. I'll be glad to go back with your partner here. Shit, with the evidence I have, I could convince even Fandano this joker is the right guy if he was blind *and* deaf," Mick insisted, wrestling with a theory, several deep-seated misgivings and a nagging perception that even if Snake did find the man, he'd never bring him back anyway.

Tagliano had admitted he'd met Ricciardi. Yet, when he'd seen him getting into his car and driving away, but for a vague description that could fit a cast of thousands, the eyewitness, the Snake-in-the-grass, never said anything that added up to much, thought Lannigan, keenly aware the man had his own reasons.

"You already know what this fellow, Ricciardi-slash-Demilo, looks like. Though, just to refresh your memory, he was the one you spotted outside my apartment building yesterday morning, if you recall," said Mick, nudging his idle hand.

Snake only glared back at the trench coat and the man in it with nothing to say.

"*Right*, anyway you could start with the swanky resorts down there. I have a suspicion he'll be trolling for new wives about now. If not, try the bars downtown, the dingy ones and the ones where the cockroaches go to feed. But wherever he is, I'm sure the parasite is working somebody's ass for a crumb in a crooked back room someplace," suggested Mick.

Tagliano continued to hang onto his silence like a piece of rope dangling from a cliff. He knew that Fandano was as hard headed as a block of granite and as stubborn as they come with a streak of depravity. He'd much rather settle for a bird in hand he could hack up than a flock of sitting ducks floating upstream he'd need to wait for. Snake couldn't see Lannigan talking his way out of too much anytime soon. Besides, taking after Ricciardi allowed him a few more options he hadn't considered. Sherlock is delivered on time. I look good doing Lannigan's dirty work if Fandano buys any of it and with my ace in the hole, I control the upper hand in both games, he determined. Maybe I will take it from here he thought, and do something I should have done a long time ago. "Since you put it that way, maybe it would be best, now that I see the big picture. I mean, let's face it, you're obviously sold on the man's guilt, and what's really important is for Mr. Fandano to get what he wants, his son's, real killer—eventually. Am I right?" he said, taking pause, glancing at Murphy and justifying his hand and his motives to all the players, including himself. "Well that's it then, but remember, you make damn sure I go down in his good books for this, and no funny business, Sherlock," Snake decreed, aware he'd most likely never see the detective again and breathing a sigh of relief. "Yeah, so long and thanks for the laughs, funny-boy. But if it happens that this doesn't work out, you know, for whatever reason, bear in mind, even bad luck has to come to an end sooner or later." He snickered.

Before leaving, Tagliano took his partner aside. "You be sure and deliver this guy to Mr. Fandano personally, *and* by midnight," ordered Snake, poking his shadow in the chest with each syllable he voiced. "I might be a while," he declared and barely above a whisper. "Tell the boss for me, I still have reservations that this Ricciardi fellow is really the man he wants, and that we've seen little proof other than some circumstantial hokey-pokey. Can you remember all that or do I have to call it in?" His associate shook his head. Snake offered a covert glance at the detective and then without another word, walked off.

"I'd ask you what that was all about," said Mick. "But you're not going to tell me and I'm terrible at charades. So listen, shadow, is it—?" said Mick. Watching Snake make his way to the ticket line, and beginning to garner a notion, he was interrupted abruptly by the man next to him.

"It's Murphy, Lannigan. The name is Murphy, goddamn it! And I'm about fed up to *here* with your smart mouth, smart-ass."

"Jesus, Murphy, you're Irish to the core for crying out loud." He grinned. "And it speaks, I feel like a proud papa. Seriously, here's the thing, Murphy," he said, dancing a jig for the man who refused to take his eyes off him. "Just in case things don't work out somehow, I thought maybe I'd like to grab a bite to eat. You know, have one truly decent, 'last meal' here in KC instead of that trash they serve in the friendly skies. What do you say, one Irishman to another? I may not have the chance when we get back, you know, with lungs being ripped out my ass, eye sockets being spooned and gutted and limbs yanked from my body like I was a giant shrimp ring and all; well admit it, a man could lose his appetite."

Murphy nodded, holding back a smile. "Go on, I'm listening."

"I was contemplating this whimsical little restaurant one of my clients told me about. You remember her? She was the blonde lying in my bed that you couldn't peel your eyes off of? Between rides on the Mickey-go-round," Mick winked at him, "she mentioned it was a favourite spot and that she'd like to take me there someday. Well, I think we can both agree that 'someday' is pretty much out of the picture for this Irishman. But we're here with some time to kill, and better it than me." He smiled. Turning around and pointing to the departures board three booths away, Lannigan continued. "We're not going anywhere anyway, Murph. The earliest flight to Conley is six-ten this evening and the Fedora Café and Bar's only a taxicab away in that direction. Come on, you Irish slug, it's plain to see you love food as much as I do." He chuckled, tapping the man's, bloated belly. "It's a saucy little bistro just down the street from that apartment building we were at on 47th. I guarantee you'll enjoy it, and if not, *hey*, shoot me." He laughed. "Thanks to your associate though, we certainly have plenty of time all of a sudden and either way, you got me. I'm not going anywhere, but we still have to eat."

"No tricks, Lannigan?"

"What are you talking about, tricks? I'm hurt. You finally learn how to string some words together and you waste them by insulting me, *ouch*, Murphy. In retrospect, I think maybe I prefer your bedside manner," he remarked, watching the man give up a grin. "I know, she put a smile on my face too," he added. "And just for the record, I'm as eager to see Fandano as your friend is to see that I do," said Mick, determined to take a detour one way or the other and finish the case he started, no matter what card Snake had up his sleeve...

Part VII

Chapter 25

The times, they are a changing for the hour's ticking down. It's just past dark in Conley and the boys were back in town. Two hard-ass Irish Catholics each from one side of the law and when—in time—their worlds collide, look what a sight the seers saw…

—9.02 p.m.—

Shortly after nine that evening, James Baldwin Murphy and Mick Lannigan found themselves back in Conley airport. Shortly after that, they were traipsing through the long, sterile halls and headed towards a parked Lincoln on the far side of the terminal as Mick noted a parallel world of silhouettes in the mirrored looking glass. Then all at once, he was able to see the foreboding Cimmerian chariot come into view along with its grim, tinted windows and contrasting chrome-plated contours. There it sat, precariously idle beyond floodlights and glass walls in the white courtesy zone, patiently waiting to collect its appointed cargo.

The detective, though, had other ideas. He wasn't quite prepared to let himself reach the vehicle or to take the scheduled ride Snake had conveniently arranged for him. Not yet anyway; it wasn't time, he figured, and he'd never been early—or even on time most likely—in his life. The more he weighed his ill-fated future, the more adamant Mick became that he wouldn't face Fandano empty-handed if he had anything to say about it. But with his .45 calibre silent partner still holed up in the dash of his car, it seemed he'd have to do his talking on another level.

Listening intently to the notion wielding its way with him, out of the corner of his eye he saw a fleeting opportunity ready to pass him by, and walking past a circular conveyer belt of luggage, gear and incoming parcels, the trench coat offered a timely comment. Ushering in a last chance once Murphy gazed over at him and then, just as quickly, looking away again, looking all the while, he readdressed the shadow's true design.

"You believe I'm innocent don't you, Murph," asked the detective in a credulous tone, hoping to redirect the man's train of thought, if only for an instant; twisting his focus and putting it back on track just long enough for Mick to do what needed to be done.

"It doesn't matter *what* I believe, Lannigan. All that matters is that Mr. Fandano is happy at the end of the day, and that's just around the next corner for you, I think. Nothing personal," he replied, staring at their chauffeured ride just past the three sets of glass doors; suddenly seeing his objective much clearer and closer, and reconsidering the significance of his answer.

Momentarily indifferent to the man flanking him, he picked up his pace towards the sliding doors, hearing the sound of hidden hydraulics open and close and watching the trickle of passengers as they came and went.

Taking advantage of Murphy's distraction and finally able to speak his mind, in one fell swoop, the detective leaned sideways. Then, like a barn owl snatching up a field mouse in its talons, he latched onto a baggage cart loaded up and bulging with suitcases two levels deep. Ripping it from the hands of its driver, Lannigan threw the teetering gurney into the stomach of the unsuspecting man at his side.

By then, the podgy Irishman had recovered from his ill-timed lapse. Turning too late however to realize what fortune had already been set in motion—and the subsequent dilemma that would befall him because of it—the avalanche of luggage struck the sinner like the elocution of a southern preacher somewhere below the bible belt as Lannigan spoke his peace. Hurled backwards with a lumbering force, Murphy was knocked over and sent tumbling along with the out-of-control, wheeled trolley as all of the bags aboard toppled onto him and, bouncing unpredictably, scattered helter-skelter, bumping, scraping and gliding aimlessly across the polished linoleum. As one piece of black, runaway Samsonite tripped up a passer-by, several more strapped satchels and a small chest rammed a bench, upending the surprised occupants.

A woman began screaming uncontrollably, perhaps startled by the unexpected happenstance or possibly it was just her own brand of upset baggage being spewed, witnessing the man-a-la-carte and watching him squirm in amongst the pile of grips as a second individual in a trench coat ran off as if a soul possessed and fleeing from the devil himself. With one hand over her mouth and stepping back unconsciously, she couldn't take her eyes off the stout-looking man in business attire flip-flopping in pathetic fashion, looking powerless against the barrage and battling to gain his footing from beneath the hefty bundles and trunks.

While the downed squab continued pitching suitcases this way and that, the detective raced out the exit. He'd postponed the inevitable for a little longer anyway, he decided, surveying the never-ending lot for a single, silver Intrepid in a late-night sea of infinite black while running faster and faster, far past the waiting sedan into the rows of parked cars. His hands rebounded off chiselled metal, glass and plastic parts and inadvertently tore a driver's side mirror from its moorings as the runner manoeuvred between them. All at once, he detected the heavy footsteps of an indignant, Irish gunman pounding the ground in back of him like a raging, wild animal on the trail of its next meal. Then, just as suddenly, they disappeared when Murphy came to an abrupt standstill out of breath and signalling for the Lincoln to pick him up.

Racing through the endless obstacles lining the acres of space, Lannigan listened to the vehicle squeal its intent as he turned to watch his destined ride drive up one row over.

Hastily breaking the opposite way, Mick realized the car wasn't moving. It had stopped in its tracks to observe his. Glancing back over his shoulder again, noticing an arm extend from the window and take careful aim, the detective saw a point of light, a flash, a revelation as a bullet ricocheted off the trunk he was, at that moment, skirting. Instinctively, much like breathing and hoping to prolong the favoured pastime, he ducked. Wincing, running even harder through the narrow and irregular openings, Lannigan continued zigzagging in and out of the mechanical maze. Still not able to see his car, he stumbled, falling to his knees and rolled into, and nearly under, the wheels of an oncoming SUV as the late model slammed on its brakes.

"Lannigan," shouted Murphy in a gruff, even flagrant tone. "I thought we had an understanding." He paused. "Well, it makes no never-mind. We can still do this easy," suggested the gunman, stepping out and away from the Lincoln. His elbow locked and the weapon pointed in the direction he'd last seen the man, spotting a Highlander farther away suddenly break with a high-priced screech for no apparent reason. "Or, we can do it *your* way," said Murphy, inching forward. "*Personally*, I'm hoping I don't have to bury a bullet in your leg or some other precious part of your anatomy just to slow you down. But, it's your choice and I'm good to go, either way." He hesitated, expanding his sway and pressing on through the cars. "So as Snake might say, 'How do you want to play this, Sherlock'?"

The detective never responded. Instead, all the time the man had been talking, Mick was scrambling on his hands and knees, back around the SUV and letting it continue on its way while he did the same.

When he felt he was out of range, Lannigan picked himself up and bolted for the far end of the lot, looking for the nearest exit that would take him out to the interstate, invariably forcing Murphy to put his gun away, get back in the car and drive around the perimeter of the lot if he had any hope at all of reaching him. However, running out of territory and his car nowhere in sight, approaching the first of six tollgates, Mick detected a lone man getting into a vehicle. Cornered at life's crossroad and with no legitimate turns left—or right—and his immediate future seemingly a dead end, he'd have to rely on inspiration to lead him out of his strait and around the next corner into the straight and narrow.

Waiting like a vulture, like a common thief in the wings under darkness for the driver to start his car, the detective found himself debating circumstance, survival, and a little further up the evolutionary ladder, conscience and ethics; even in the poor lighting, it was obvious Mick just might come up a few rungs short on this night, but then being pursued by a crazed gunman he couldn't respond to in kind made the decision a whole lot easier. With his ivory-handled mouthpiece still out of reach, he was soundly overmatched and sincerely understated. The low road didn't seem to be an issue suddenly, not as long as he had something to drive away in, he decided. All that really mattered was a ready mode of travel—whether it was a Ford Focus or not, he determined—listening to the four-door Continental weaving its way around the three acres of park-and-fly to get to him.

Flinging the door open and jumping in the passenger's side the minute the engine turned over, Lannigan snatched the bearded owner from behind the wheel. Then taking him by the scruff of the collar, he dragged him across the front seat and tossed him out the same door he himself entered from.

"Sorry, fellow," mumbled the detective, watching the man tumble out of the car and landing awkwardly on the pavement by Mick's feet. "I know it doesn't seem like it from where you're sitting at the moment, but I'm doing you a favour. This is a Ford, after all," Mick said, starting to climb in as the young man scrambled to pick himself up, reacting to the attack and willing to protect his property. "*Uh*," barked the detective. "Now you see," said Lannigan, feigning a weapon under his coat and reaching inside to retrieve it, "if you're not careful, you're going to make me do something you won't have a chance to regret later." He watched the owner of the vehicle, a shorter man in his mid-to-late twenties, glance away as a diamond-studded earring caught the light and twinkled off his lobe. The detective withdrew his hand and, getting in, pulled the passenger door shut behind him. Staying put, the young, dark-haired, car-jack victim never made a move until Lannigan had driven off.

With a brief squeal of tires, in his haste, the departing car thief scraped the fender of the next vehicle over, a Ford Bronco, as he drove from the slot. Kissing cousins he mused, speeding up and checking the rear-view mirror, aware of just how close Murphy was all of a sudden.

Taking the turn into a feeder lane only a short distance from the exit to the gate and misjudging, Lannigan managed to clip another vehicle with his front bumper. Hearing the crunch of metal resounding in the darkness, he unexpectedly witnessed the left-side headlamp rupture—fuelled and fused like a dying miniature nova—as it crackled, fizzled and finally dispersed in the half-light. Reeling from the backlash and bouncing between parked cars like a pinball under the control of a demonic wizard, the detective exploded through the gate onto the interstate watching painted slats of timber and thick, clear plastic shatter and fly off in all directions.

Jamming the gearshift into overdrive, he accelerated into traffic with his foot to the floor, his heart in his throat and his conscience riding his tail harder than the Lincoln less than a few hundred yards behind, and both beginning to eliminate the discrepancy.

As the two vehicles approached the outskirts of the city, Lannigan suddenly heard weapons blazing while the borrowed, white Focus took a barrage of gunfire from Murphy and his driver.

In only a few short moments they had succeeded in reshaping the rear of the stolen vehicle, bursting the back window and shredding the tires till one of them was all but sheared from its rim.

He knew full well he was quickly running out of time; the gas tank in back of him ignited, annihilating the rear frame and jettisoning the bumper, along with the panel beneath it, into the air as the back end erupted in flames. At the same instant, the impact threw him hard against the steering wheel, causing the horn to sound. Instinctively pushing, grabbing the handle and flinging the door open, Lannigan leapt from the fiery inferno while it was still moving. Seconds before the bullet-riddled and flaming Ford crashed into the side of a nearby pickup parked at the curb, the detective struck the ground, landing on his shoulder and, like an oversized bowling ball inside a well-worn tan-colored raincoat, rolled across the asphalt towards the very collision he'd incited.

With the black sedan closing fast, and seeing several apartment buildings along the street, Mick ran for the entrance directly in front of him. Nearing the steps, he tripped as the Lincoln drove up. Scuffing along on all fours, pawing the risers and runners until he could negotiate his balance and get to his feet again, his momentum carried him headfirst into the glass door. Quickly reaching up and fumbling for the handle, he opened it and entered the empty foyer. As the glass door behind him closed, Murphy fired a single shot that fractured the entranceway and caused the shards of debris to rain in on him. With the inside entry locked, he threw himself against the wall out of the line of fire expecting, and waiting for, another. Then, catching a glimpse of a shadow getting out of the car beneath a streetlight just up ahead of the blaze, Mick heard a second shot ricochet off the inside of the metal doorframe.

Trapped, anxious and desperate, he began pushing the buttons on a security panel. "It's me, baby, I'm back. Open up, gorgeous," he repeated over and over, each time he pressed the numbered squares on the wall-mounted board. Lannigan's reasoning led him to believe somebody would surely be waiting for a husband, lover or boyfriend. He only needed one taker. If it should happen to be a man at the other end, he presumed the fellow—suspicious just by the greeting—would be even more willing to let him in.

"Open up, gorgeous, it's me," he went on, all at once noticing Murphy break into a full stride up the walk towards him with his gun in hand.

Suddenly, the buzzer on the door started droning its approval in terms he could appreciate. An endless clamour of white noise resounded inside the small chamber as he yanked open the entryway, stepped inside and quickly disappeared from Murphy's sights. Listening to the glass door being shattered by a third comment from the pursuer's outspoken, though limited vocabulary echoing his frustration, the detective immediately took one of the available elevators and, applying his previous technique to gain entry, pressed every number on the bank of buttons while waiting for the doors to close. Seconds later, it was moving. Shortly after that, it jerked to a stop and Mick Lannigan stepped out onto an empty second floor.

Cognizant that the man would be following the elevator's progress, he slipped into the stairwell at the end of the hall, descended the stairs and, reaching the main floor again, able to see Murphy through the window of the exit door, Lannigan left the building. He ran off down a back alley towards the street, already looking for a cab even before the elevator made its final stop on the seventh landing.

With all the damage that had been introduced to the courtyard outside, Murphy knew the police would be out to investigate long before Lannigan ever showed his face. Putting his gun away and determining any more effort would be futile for the time being, James Murphy returned to the car.

Moments after the black sedan drove off, turning a corner at the end of the roadway, a police cruiser pulled up alongside the remains of the burning Ford.

An officer got out.

Seeing no one around and looking puzzled at the vision of a sedate neighborhood with an abandoned car, and now a pickup truck, in flames in the middle of it, the sergeant removed his hat, scratched his head and then casually, reaching inside his vehicle, notified the fire department; though, upon closer inspection during his call, he also detected the bullet-riddled shell of the white wagon and decided to call for backup.

Driving through the projects lining the route deeper into Conley, and with only a little over two hours till midnight, Murphy decided to play a hunch.

Conscious of the detective's conviction and now his tenacity, and not being too far from the airport to begin with, he was willing to gamble everything that Lannigan would be heading for Cancún himself— sooner or later. That's what this had been all about, he determined, tapping his driver on the shoulder. "All right, back to the airport, Salvo," he ordered, staring out the window into the darkened streets; realizing the late hour, based on a timepiece he decided to check once more, and coming to understand the resourcefulness of the detective, Murphy began wondering if he was up to the task and just what it meant if he wasn't.

Ready to give up after almost four hours, the two witnessed their trench coat step out of a red and white taxi. Watching the cab drive off, Lannigan took a sweeping glance around the entrance of the terminal, turned and, seeing no one he wanted to, went inside.

Like a mugging back in those very same projects they'd cruised earlier in the evening, Murphy and his chauffeur, Salvo Coppola, apprehended their flat-footed runaway two hundred yards from an Air Canada ticket window near one in the morning. Tackling his fugitive, the Irishman slammed the other to the ground, driving the face of the trench coat into the unforgiving marble floor. Sandwiched between a rock and a hard place, Mick exhaled a loud, lung-clearing moan while the crack of his skull competed for volume. Lying motionless and in a daze, his patter was finally put to rest, tongue-tied at the hands of Fandano's two henchmen.

Straddling the detective, Murphy quickly presented a pair of manacles. And like a steer being roped before it was branded, while the driver introduced the side of Lannigan's head to his size eleven, Italian shoe leather, Murphy whipped the man's arms, limp and near lifeless, up from the flat of the chequered surface and smartly, anxiously, handcuffed his quarry...

Chapter 26

In a warehouse on the I-state, they were meeting once again. So would it be his new beginning or just beginning of the end? While he stood to face Fandano and the cuffs fell from his wrist, it suddenly occurred to him, the rattled Snake produced his own sub-plot and yet another, little twist. Yes, Mick realized his nexus at precisely two oh nine and how Snake had roiled his own sweet sinister, sadistic story line...

—SATURDAY, MAY 8th—2. 09a.m.—

Shown little mercy, Mick Lannigan was hoisted from the cold, crippling floor of the terminal like an oyster being ripped from its jimmied shell, like a stock-still raggedy Andy doll—roughed up and teetering on the edge of unconsciousness—after he was restrained.

As they hauled the battered and bruised fugitive to his feet, Mick struggling just to stand, a security guard approached, attempting to intervene. The driver quietly called the man over while shrewdly drawing a weapon from his inside coat pocket. Then, plying it neatly into the guard's ribs when he was close enough, Salvo pointed out to the uniformed intruder that they were just leaving and that he might strongly consider doing the same. "And unless you'd care for a taste of this fellow's bout with a bad day," he whispered, grumbling into the guard's ear. "I suggest you do an about face, *and* your job by breaking up that rowdy mob you've let get out of hand there," he said in a stern pitch, grinning as he tucked the pistol seamlessly, even artfully, into its sheath.

Backing away, immediately dismissing himself and announcing that everything was well in hand, massaging the bruised flesh where the barrel had been, the young airport watchman walked off to a nearby lunchroom. There, instead of a gun, he'd face a steaming cup of hot coffee flavoured with a stiff drink in it to cut the chill in his bones, the temperature of the brew, and the adrenaline filling his head with a sobering truth that scared the life out of him.

As the gawking throng began to slowly disperse, the flaccid man in the tan-coloured trench coat, in his muddled state, was promptly escorted to the Lincoln on the other side of the throughway three rows in, next to a lamppost marked 'B-3'.

Out of patience, time and any thought of goodwill, Murphy continued his assault, manhandling the detective out the exit and across the street. Reaching the sedan, he hurled Lannigan into the side panel of the trunk while he opened the rear door. Then, grabbing the man by his hair, Murphy tossed his cargo head first inside. Striking his face on the far door handle, Mick rolled off the seat, fell to the floor and waited helplessly to be rescued as he conceded to the assault and finally blacked out.

Already several hours past their deadline, the trio drove back to the industrial district not far up the highway, overlooking the much-maligned Hudson River.

There was no blindfold when Mick came around. Only Fandano's plans blurring his vision while he mulled over, and reasoned out, an alternate notion—a long shot on the short, shotgun ride, he mused—that he found most disturbing and serpentine. He toyed with Snake's likely connection from the very beginning and long before he'd come into the picture, and the frame, the work of art merrily painted by the master with so many shades of wrong if he was right. Had Murphy knocked some sense into him he debated, flinching from the pain rattling around his head. Perhaps! Because suddenly, there were just too many anomalies, too many issues that created more questions than they answered. Each one brought Lannigan back to the man that had yanked him from his warm, cozy blonde-filled bed and who ultimately altered his life forever only days before.

Everything happens for a reason he deliberated and, just as true, nothing happens without one either. That was Snake in the flesh. Scales, fork-tongue, rattle and all, thought the detective, reviewing his litany of circumstantial evidence and a seed starting to take root in the pit of his belly—a gut feeling that grabbed him like a bout of uncontrollable, runaway diarrhea because his large, hairy-knuckled Italian didn't seem like the type who'd waste a breath, or a moment of his time, and fly off half-cocked for anyone but himself. Certainly not to prolong the life of a two-bit, penny-ante, poker-playing, nickel-and-dime Sherlock or, even more to the point, to chase down someone he never considered a legitimate prospect in the first place according to him. And what did all that mean to Mick Lannigan? It meant plenty! It meant Snake was after something more.

No, he decided, feeling the cuffs digging in and gnawing away at the flesh and bones beneath them while his ride approached the warehouse of the Acme Trucking Company. That was wrong, he debated. Snake was after more than the obvious. He was after much more. In fact, Paul Alfonso Tagliano was in it up to his neck *and*, *after it all*, the detective reeled, his eyes blown wide open as if he'd just been blindsided by a two-by-four across the back of the head, experiencing an epiphany of sorts.

Inside, Fandano was getting restless, and had been since well before midnight, pacing the floor, listening to his thoughts and the hum of fans whirl overhead while he was forced to smoke another "cheap *fucking* cigar," he grumbled. He sensed his patience dwindling down faster even than the poorly rolled Cohiba he was rolling back and forth in his mouth. As the man changed direction, retracing his steps the other way, he heard a thud when the door behind him swung open.

Two men entered.

"You're a day late," he said, uncommonly calm given his mood. "Fortunately, I blame the man with you and the other one who apparently isn't," declared Fandano, assessing circumstance, an explanation and presuming that Tagliano would be joining them shortly. "I also see you came empty-handed so to speak," he went on. "Still, I guess I have my answer, don't I, detective?"

"I realize this looks incriminating based on your expectations, but I wouldn't jump to any conclusions if I were you, at least not till you hear me out," remarked Lannigan with a composure and sedate tone that surprised even him.

"If I were you, I wouldn't be telling *me* what I should and shouldn't be doing. And I certainly wouldn't have shown up without a warm body in my hot little hands to take the heat off."

"Arriving this way wasn't my first choice, believe me," he mumbled, looking pensive while the worry lines rumbled across his forehead.

"Maybe not, but it looks like it will be your last," he said, flipping the cigar between his fingers before taking a long draw. "And since we're speaking truths, you surprise me, Lannigan. You weren't *my* first choice either; however, I'm in the better position to be disappointed, I suppose. And one way or the other, I end up with what I want, and what my son deserves… justice!"

"Right," Mick conceded, droning his response, wanting to say more, but holding off till the pounding in his skull subsided. "*Justice*, yeah that's the word I was hunting for." He paused. "Sure, I'm here. Have your perverted sense of closure if that's all you want from this, this hypocrisy you call *justice*. I've no doubt you could justify everything without too much trouble and declare your conscience clear. Why not, after all, you're calling the shots anyway." He stumbled, almost losing his nerve. "*Hell*, execute whoever you want, go ahead. Decide on a whim that I destroyed your son's life and then as usual, wash your hands of the whole, damn thing," he submitted, studying the man's face watching his. "Who'd be the wiser, not your son. *No*, but *you* would, and you'd have to live with that every day, and forever. Something tells me you're better than that, and you'd prefer to do this right, if it's possible," said Lannigan in a tone suggesting it was. "Do you want an answer based on truth and fact, or *time*? I believe you'd rather get your hands on the real culprit. Let Frank rest in peace knowing why, and that you did him right every step of the way. Honour the Omerta, and his memory …" stated Lannigan in a softer voice, detecting a hint of sensibility, and perhaps even tolerance, on Fandano's face, "instead of taking the easy way out. No one respects anybody who gets it like that. You're no different, even if it is your own kind of justice in the end."

"Is that a fact, Lannigan?" said Fandano, his rejoinder completely unruffled.

"I think so," replied the detective.

"And Snake would be where exactly, and even more to the point, isn't here *why*?" he inquired waving his hands in small circles, looking at Murphy and then back at Lannigan.

"You know, that's a *damn* good question when you get right down to it. I do know where he's supposed to be. We both do; though, when it comes down to what he's actually doing, I suspect I know a little more than your man, Murphy, here."

"Well then, why don't we start with that," suggested his judge, jury and self-appointed executioner.

"I believe he's stalking your son's true killer, but for very different reasons. He agreed to fly to Cancún in my place—something about time restraints—and bring this fellow back," offered Lannigan, sounding insincere in his estimation of the part-time bounty hunter.

"But I have my doubts, and *serious* ones. My gut says otherwise; still, I don't have much else to substantiate it. Though what I do have is this notion gnawing at me that he's somehow involved in far more than meets the eye. Like say, having a hand in your son's death," he professed, contemplating Fandano's reaction. "It's a recurring theme that tugs at me like a noose around my neck, or my *balls* in your version."

"*What*? You're insane! Snake's like a brother, *a son* to me! No, that's ludicrous," he said, not sure what to think and then all at once, curious about the man's rationale. "Why?" he asked, almost whispering. His face furrowed and his eyes squinting as he glared at the detective.

"I admit that beyond the obvious, I haven't got much, but there's always a reason. Maybe he was afraid your son would change his mind and step up to the family business. Or even break your spirit, have you step down while applying that earlier sentiment of yours. Grief-stricken, you take a fade while someone else you favour," Mick hesitated, "conveniently takes over. From the get-go, he was eager to keep tabs on me. But then the closer I came to solving your son's murder, the closer he stuck to me, till the only difference between him and my own shadow was his malice breathing down my neck like pine tar gumming up the works. It's almost as if he's been playing both ends from the middle the whole time. Killing two birds, and one accomplice, with a single stone he can hurl at will from under everyone's nose. He knows at midnight, if I can't convince you I'm an innocent in all of this, I'll be the newest resident of the Hudson out there. Even if he does bring the man back—and that's a *damn* big 'if', enormous in fact—where's the proof you need to validate his guilt? Why, it's safe and sound at the bottom of the river… with what's left of me. A few well-worded details from your serpent, Snake, the man walks, *they both do*, and who's the wiser? It's too pat," said the Irishman. "And to use a remark he made, too easy all round, like I say, if he even brings the son-of-a-bitch back at all. For the record, my money's on your man tying up loose ends with a well-placed stone, but again, that's just a hunch."

"Go on," demanded the Sicilian, his cold, deadpan cresol eyes changing their appearance. "Finish it, what are you saying?"

"I'm saying there's a lot more going on than just murder," proclaimed Lannigan as he noticed Murphy stepping forward. "And that you don't have to be a detective to find a knife in your back, especially if it's in your own backyard. Shit's everywhere! The only question now is which way is the fan pointing and whose face will it end up on?"

"Could I have a word with you, Mr. Fandano?" asked the gunman. The man called him over with two fingers. Murphy obliged immediately while Lannigan waited and watched.

"Snake, umm," he mumbled, "wanted me to inform you of a few things, Mr. Fandano," he began.

After a minute or two, Murphy was dismissed, as G. Luciano Fandano made an about-face gazing off past his desk and deliberating over what he'd heard. He slowly turned back around and, before speaking, stared at Lannigan for a moment. "I'm suddenly intrigued,

Detective. Spell it out for me," ordered Fandano, more interested in the man's direction and his own new perspective, given Tagliano's message.

"Spell it out?"

"Yeah, and use *big* letters."

"You're a smart man; you must be to have gotten where you are, and to stay there as long as you have." Mick faltered, thinking about his argument and wondering if it would delay the inevitable or put him on a fast track to it. "Dot your 'I's for a start—*Snake* eyes. Then cross the 'T's. You might as well, he *double-crossed* his, and that's why I'm here, I'll wager; so all that's left is to fill in those pesky, little blanks. But consider this, whose idea was it to include the Irishman?" He paused, locking eyes with his accuser. "And there it is. The look on your face tells me all I need to know. I think maybe it's time to face another, not so pleasant, reality."

"Shut *the hell* up, Lannigan," bellowed Fandano raising his fist, then opening it and rolling it over as if he might slap the detective with the back of his hand. He recalled a conversation he'd had with Tagliano and the one Lannigan was referring to.

"Make up your mind, but the spelling lesson's not over. Besides, if I keep my mouth shut, I'm as good as dead anyway. I have nothing to lose, but we—both of us—have everything to gain. So no, Mr. Fandano, I'm not going to shut *the hell* up," said Mick boldly, beginning to see the man as the flawed character he was turning into right before his eyes. "You tasked me to do a job. Well I usually finish what I start and, for starters, I know precisely who murdered your son. More importantly, so does Snake, and believe me when I say it *was* murder. Callous and completely calculated," he whispered. "From all accounts, the man you're after, amongst a slew of other things, is a suspected wife killer," Mick went on. "He's been planning the death of his present one up to about yesterday, mid-morning I'd say, when he suddenly discovered who else he'd killed besides his ex in that explosion on March tenth; his ex being Adella Hughes, the other victim in his heinous, little scheme to rid the world of a circling albatross." He paused, not sure the man would even accept his truth no matter how compelling the argument was. "You see, she'd jilted him, Adella—her husband, not your son. At the outset, I figured it was a lover's scorn festering in his twisted, little brain like a recessive gene in the Ozarks, or a malignant tumour eating him up. Then I examined the insurance angle. And maybe that was even the case, but now, now I get the distinct impression there's more to it and that it involved Frank all along …" He hesitated intentionally, "when worlds began to suddenly collide—yours, my female client's, Adella Hughes and then mine."

"I don't follow, and what the hell does any of this have to do with my son, or Pauly anyway?" he groused, raising his voice; losing his patience and latching onto another Coronas Especiales from a nearby humidor.

"My client is his *third* wife, though she's making every effort to change that blunder. She showed up on my doorstep with an insurance policy that she didn't know anything about until recently, claiming her husband was trying to do her in. Antelo Pilattzi was his name when he married her, alias somebody else during his second marriage lasting all of a week and a half, alias Tony Scalatto who just happened to be Adella Hughes' husband." All at once, Fandano looked sincerely interested in what the detective was trying to impose on him. "Now you could wait for a court of law to sort it all out, but there's no way you're going to do that. Or you can take my word for it based on the evidence I've gathered. You have to agree," said Mick, feeling like he was winning the man over, "I've nothing to gain here except my life." Fandano grinned, and then let out a laugh as the whirs and whines of the fans above them were silenced by his guffaw.

"You're a pistol, Lannigan—a chip off the old block, balls as big as a fist, indeed. I'm starting to think it would be a shame to do away with you." He hesitated, lighting his cigar and having trouble. "Continue," he said, still trying to light it.

"Well the thing is, Adella was his first wife like I said, but she left before… anyway she left the guy— smart move on her part. Lucky for a time, but once destiny's set in motion, not even you and all *your* influence can change the course it takes. It swings like a pendulum and the only thing that can stop it is its conclusion. Initially, in fact right up to this afternoon, I thought your son was an innocent bystander in all of this, an untimely mistake on the part of this twisted son-of-a-bitch.

However, now I have this pestering doubt in my gut, like a red-hot coal burning a hole in my colon, that Snake scripted this misadventure from the very beginning. It's either a damn good hunch or it was planted there by that frigging jalapeño pepper I gagged on yesterday," reported Lannigan. "Here's your proof," he said, slowly reaching into his trench coat as Murphy's gun moved closer to Lannigan's abdomen, "a copy of the receipt from a gun shop where the man bought the explosives just up the street here in Conley. I've got a witness, your Pauly as a matter of fact, that saw the man leaving my apartment after he tried to kill me because I was interfering with the plans he had to kill his latest wife, my other client. There's a car rental agency that will back that up. I also have a woman by the name of Katrina Goodhue that this fellow was seeing—but as Vincent Demilo—who insists he regularly rambled on about blowing the shit out of certain individuals that had ruined his life. Meaning Adella, I suppose, possibly for leaving him." Mick paused, attempting to decipher Fandano's face. "I have more, including several phone messages from a civilian in the 52nd Precinct corroborating everything I've just told you," he said, taking a breath. "So the man you want isn't me, Mr. Fandano. The man you want to get your hands on, to start with anyway, is Lonzo Ricciardi. As for Snake bringing him back, I don't think he'll have too much luck," said Lannigan, unaware of just how accurate he was. "As for the rest of it, you can question Snake whenever he gets around to showing up."

"Demilo, another alias?" inquired Fandano, still piecing the puzzle together.

"That's right, his latest from what I can tell and I have a stinking suspicion, his last," the detective concluded, "one way or the other."

The man holding the cigar placed it in his mouth, cupped his hands together behind his back and, with a pensive stare, gazed up at the ceiling watching the fans spin as the smoke from the heater was drawn towards them. After more than a full minute of silence, Fandano removed the cigar and looked back at his bird in hand.

"For the time being anyway, until I get Tagliano's side of things, I'm giving you a free pass. But I know where you live, detective and for how long, remember that! I'm never farther away than a stray bullet, a car accident or an incidental conclusion to an otherwise bad day. If you're lucky, being Irish, you won't ever see me again, because if you do, it won't be your best *fucking* day, my friend, just your last... bad one." He hesitated, looking Lannigan up and down. "The driver will take you wherever you want to go. Let's hope it's a safe destination and a one-way trip." He grinned, blowing a stream of smoke through the air as he walked off.

Lannigan didn't say a word as Murphy escorted him out the door of the warehouse, willing only to embrace his reprieve quietly. He'd have time later to celebrate with a tall bottle of Napoleon brandy and a poker game downstairs at the Mayflower.

Fandano strolled around the desk, sat down and, picking up the receiver, watched the two men leave.

"I wish I could say it was a pleasure, Murphy, but the fact is I neither have the inclination nor the time," Lannigan admitted, conscious it might take a while to get cleaned up for his next appointment and, at the same time, examining a prominent bump on the back of his head with a gentle stroke of his hand. "You see, I have another funeral to attend later this morning and the only good news is, it isn't *mine*," he said, ducking down before sliding into the back seat of the jet-black Lincoln...

Chapter 27

Somewhere way down in Cancún, two men would ride the story out, each fearful of the other and of that, there's little doubt. Ricciardi played his cards straight up the way they'd been revealed, while the man who had arranged the game, knew either way, his fate was sealed. So on a late night in the islands, they acted out their final hand, confronting one another face to face, and man to man. The rivals drew their weapons, without a word, without a sound. Just like a sack of pinball hammers, one took a bullet 'twixt the eyes and in a hush, fell to the ground...

It was the following day when a half-dozen of Fandano's thugs arrived at Cancún International Airport. With the information received on an anonymous tip even before reaching the island, they were quickly able to locate the whereabouts of a body near the Royal Sands Resort; however, they were surprised to discover the dead man was Paul Tagliano, and Fandano's second. But for the massive hole in the frontal lobe of Snake's skull, there was no way of telling his premature demise in a back alley was brought to a head for double-crossing the same man who was meant to hand him the brass ring. Instead though, he was issued a cold piece of lead to mark the occasion.

It took them a little longer to round up Lonzo Ricciardi, who was hiding out in a notorious gin joint on the other side of the island.

Shortly before nightfall, the group of seven were leaving the northeast tip of the Yucatan Peninsula—overlooking the Caribbean Sea, vaunting its turquoise waters and white sands—with their goods conveniently tucked away.

Leaving Snake's body exactly where they'd found it, and drugging Ricciardi before loading his, and the casket it was bundled up in, onto the plane, they returned to the Continental United States.

In a few short hours, their imported freight would face his executioner for the first and final time. The duce that promised heads would roll, and verily burn, was never in doubt that he'd get his ounce of justice and pound of flesh one way or the other.

Presenting the coffin and propping it upright before Fandano, who was anxiously getting to his feet, they pried the lid open, listening to the ache of wood and wire nails. The head-hunter, considering the contents within, was finally able to see the man responsible for his son's demise, bound and gagged and strapped to the frame, squirming like a swarm of maggots on a hellish day. Entangled and writhing uncontrollably over a piece of rotting fruit and, still Fandano mused, it was nothing compared to what would be. Stepping closer to the creature inside moaning and mumbling his circumstance, the grief-stricken father slowly bared his teeth and, with the fury of a wounded beast, drove his fist into the man's mid-section. He watched Ricciardi buckle as far as the restraints would allow, and embracing his pathetic whines, the Sicilian head-hunter stepped back to light a cigar. Gloating over his prey like a proud lion before he played the life out of it, feeding his soul, he tortured the peculiar prize inside the oddly-shaped crackerjack box to death.

Like Dickens' Scrooge, the quite deranged and salacious G. Luciano Fandano was better than his word. Then quietly disposing of the remains in the nearby Hudson, he departed the Acme storage facility for what would be the last time, savouring the bittersweet dregs of one more chapter in his life drawing to an end. Satisfied that he had found his closure, albeit a hollow vengeance, he was heartsick and even haunted by what he knew, witnessing the torched warehouse below him explode in flames and spread like wildfire…

Chapter 28

In a smoky little bar way down on Palladin this day, there was a quiet rendezvous for neither one could stay away. Yes, at a table in the corner where they'd been but once before, they reminisced, two passing ships, one endless night and nothing more...

—4.15 p.m.—

Finding himself at the Mayflower a few minutes late, Mick Lannigan strolled over to a table near the corner down in back.

Without any exchange, and seeing the twosome from behind the bar, Skully delivered a wine-spritzer and a brandy neat to the couple.

"Thanks, my friend—and a triple, no less! It appears I have expensive taste after all. And apparently you read minds as well as you write them," said the detective, winking. The barkeep nodded, grinning back and forth at the pair while Mick quenched his thirst. Then, staring at the drink a moment, admiring the glass and rotating it from side to side, between his thumb and forefingers, the man in the tan trench coat sampled another sip before putting it down. "I have to tell you, it's been a nerve-racking forty-eight hours; but seeing you there, and me here able to appreciate you there, it was almost worth it." He paused, watching the blonde slowly remove a cigarette from a pack of Export 'A', light it and take a long draw that drew his attention. She quietly placed it in the ashtray. "What now, Miss Carlisle?" asked Lannigan, lifting his drink towards hers and recalling a previous meeting as their glasses kissed. "Now that we both have our lives back, what's next?"

She smiled, putting her spritzer down, brushing her hair out of her eyes and gazing deep into his. "The truth is nothing's changed, Mick. I'm still looking for a husband," she confessed, smiling her warmest one— remembering their first conversation and not all that long ago. Watching him intimately, she waited for a response.

"Well, don't look at me, and *especially* not like that," he replied, taking a mouthful, and then another. "Granted, the dealer hasn't finished with me yet, but so far you're not in the cards, good-looking." He hesitated. "Besides, you can do better than the likes of me, a two-bit, Irish dragon slayer with more luck than brains."

"I don't think so, Mick. No, I don't; so maybe I'll just stick around a little while longer and ignore that poker face you're suddenly wearing like a cheap suit you wouldn't be caught dead in. Experience tells me we're good together. It also says that I should call your bluff and have you lay *all* your cards on the table."

"Experience marks nothing more than time I'm afraid, lovely lady."

"But each time has its place," she said, noticing his eyes caress her features and swallow them up like a hungry man hunting down his next meal.

"True; and each one of those places is a world of its own, Cassie."

"That's right, yours and mine, Mickey. Colliding head over heels amongst the stars in a galaxy we can claim, and stealing a little piece of heaven on the way by. What do you say, handsome?"

"I say it was a nice place to visit, gorgeous and, yes, even a little piece of heaven for a short while. Unfortunately, I think our worlds are just too different." He stumbled, mesmerized by her full, pouting, red lips wrapped around the end of her cigarette. "So I say it's time for a fresh deck and a new dealer." He smiled, looking up his sleeve and, finding it empty, decided to throw in his hand. She listened sadly, surprised and speechless. "Sorry beautiful, no dice this time; my gambling days are behind me. But we get our lives back, you and I. That's not a bad deal after all. Me, I'm moving on. It's time, I think. Don't get me wrong, I'm grateful. I owe you a lot, Cassie, and I won't soon forget it! *Hell*, you probably saved my life coming into it when you did. Which reminds me, here's your ring," he said, pulling the bauble from a pocket.

Taking it with a puzzled look on her face, Cassandra Carlisle examined it. "Where did you get *this*?"

"I found it, on the floor of my apartment when I came to the other day. You must've dropped it," he suggested.

"I never had it with me. Before I left the apartment in Kansas City, I took it off my finger and threw it at the bastard," she said, passing it back to Mick.

Picking up the shiny trinket, examining it in the light, he suddenly concluded who'd trashed his place. For whatever reason, Demilo had gone back to look for it.

"Well," she said getting up from the table and putting out her cigarette, "you know what you're missing, and if you ever change your mind, hard-ass, you know how to find me, *right*, you're a detective after all," she stammered, feeling awkward because of the look he was giving her. "So take care, Mr. Lannigan, you're quite the dragon slayer, as advertised."

Mick tipped his hat and watched her leave, smiling to himself, wondering if he was making the right decision. Downing his drink, he contemplated it—and the rest of his life—giving the lady enough time to fade into the world outside the Mayflower before he did.

In the meantime, there he sat, thoroughly convinced that if every card hadn't fallen just the way it did, he wouldn't be there to read the winning hand lying on the table in front of him as he rolled the ring around in his fingers. Like a house of cards, remove any one and what happens? It collapses. Its form buckles and the whole thing falls in on itself. If not for Jack's death, Cassie coming into his life just then, opportunity knocking his door down, being suspected of murder, Snake's untimely aspirations or simply taking the book over a bauble at Kat's apartment, like that house, he wouldn't be still standing either, thought the detective. Getting up, Lannigan left as well, walking back to his place and the world he'd chosen instead of other pursuits...

Part VIII

Chapter 29

Right or wrong is not the issue, but is indeed, what most perceive, so a victim of a circumstance is very easy to believe. And in the case of this detective where all the fingers point his way, just remember who was handed what, and had a hand in what they had to say…

—SATURDAY, MAY 22ⁿᵈ—1.00 p.m.—

Two weeks later, Lannigan was rummaging through his closet for a pair of pants when he heard a knock at the door. Before he could respond, whoever it was pounded again, this time with a more pronounced and persistent rap. At the same moment the resonant voice yelled their urgency, the frame of the door detached from its hinges and fell inward, crashing to the floor in front of the visitor. Tossing his trousers, hanger and all, on the bed at the back of him, the detective raced down the hall to see what the commotion was all about. With his .45 already drawn and pointed towards the entrance, Mick watched the lone intruder make his way inside. First standing on top, and then stepping around the hole-ridden panel, he wore a cocky smile on his face and a badge in the palm of his hand.

"*Stern*, what the hell do you want now?" said Lannigan, lowering his weapon and beginning to place it back in its shoulder holster.

"Good call," declared Stern, seeing the Irishman start to slide the piece away. "But I'll take that if you don't mind. As you've no doubt guessed by my tone and this shield, I'm here on official business, and this time it's going to stick, Mr. *Detective*."

"Apparently you get a perverse pleasure from irritating the shit out of me. Give me a few days, and I'll look into getting you a life, or at least a hobby you might be good at. So what is it I've done this time that would cause you to, quite literally, break down my door and put a grin that wide on such an ugly puss?"

"Still shooting off your mouth—and firing blanks at that, eh, smart-ass. You know I look at you and I can't be sure which end is up sometimes, Lannigan." He laughed. "No matter, but we are going to be using my rules for a change this time. Now hand that Colt over before I decide to add resisting arrest *and assault* to the murder charge."

"Is this some kind of sick, twisted joke, Stern? Because it isn't the least bit funny."

"Lieutenant Stern to you," he snarled. "And it's no joke. You're just a little confused is all because of the smile on my face," he said. "It seems a passer-by found Lonzo Ricciardi's body, well a piece of it anyway, when it washed up on the shore of the Hudson River outside of Delray. A hand to be precise and a string of aliases as long as his arm ..." he chuckled, "as well, along with it. Even with the decomposition, the prints were enough to identify its late owner. And given your recent history, the fact that you've been shacking up with his widow, well, the rest was easy. I suppose you could say all fingers point to you." Stern grinned, and then just as quickly, let it fade. "You have the right to remain silent," he rhymed off. "Anything you say ..." he continued while Mick Lannigan considered his situation, the consequences and the fact that remaining silent was his only option—if he knew what was good for him.

"Next stop, a holding cell at the 52nd, then I can finally wash my hands of filth like you while I still have them. I've wasted enough time," remarked the lieutenant, preparing to cuff him.

"Listen, you don't need those. I'm not going to give you any more trouble."

"Sure, and the next thing you know, I wake up in so many pieces stuffed inside a dumpster out near the highway," he replied, slapping the shackles on anyway before leading him out into the hallway. "I always knew, deep down, you had a dark streak that would give you away one day; but I never thought you were the type to mutilate husbands who got in the way of a little slap and tickle. There's no telling what some people are capable of when it comes to the fairer sex," said Stern, shaking his head and shoving Lannigan into the elevator...

Chapter 30

If it's cops and crime and chaos you have an interest in, then welcome to the cell of Brice Michael Lannigan. But not for long my wayward friend if you can find a quarter-mil, I know it's hard to swallow; in fact, it's quite the precious pill. However, someone did step forward and for now you're free to go. Yes, you've either twisted someone's ear, or it's not what, but who you know…

—SUNDAY, MAY 23rd—8.00 a.m.—

As an officer inserted a key into the padlock, Lannigan, hearing the metallic sounds of steel on steel, stirred from his deep sleep. Disoriented for a moment, recalling a nightmare that was even more vivid, awake all of a sudden, the detective rolled over, staring up at a solitary man in uniform unlocking his temporary lodgings buried deep in the bowels of the 52nd Precinct.

"Let's go, Lannigan," ordered the young officer, sliding the cell door open. The prisoner swung around on the flimsy trundle bed and sat up.

"Go where?" he asked in a sluggish and suspicious tone, grabbing his coat off the end of the cot, though in no great hurry and checking the pockets before remembering he didn't need to.

"That's up to you. All I know is what the chief tells me and he said somebody covered your bail," offered the corporal, watching the man put on his trench coat. "You can pick up your personal belongings at the front desk and then you're free to go."

"Really, *free*? I can leave—just like that." Mick hesitated, wondering who he knew that had that kind of money to throw around. Then much like the morning sun rising over the city of Delray, it suddenly dawned on him as well and, in the moment, he considered why.

"Just like that," repeated the officer.

"Dammit! It's a shame Stern isn't here for my coming-out party. I know how much he would've hated it." He smiled, sliding the cell door closed behind him. Walking past the man in blue, Lannigan headed towards the stairs leading to the main floor, then the front desk and, down the hall, the light of day at the end of the tunnel, all at once realizing what he'd known all along...

EPILOGUE

'Somehow they stayed that way, for those 'Five Days in May', made all the stars around them shine. Funny how you can look in vain, living on nerves and such sweet pain, the loneliness that cuts so fine, to find the face you've seen a thousand times...' And on that final note, there's very little left to say except that love is really nothing till you give it all away...

—FRIDAY, MAY 28th-—AROUND 10.00 p.m.—

Neither one had left the other's side for close to a week. Not since he'd been released from jail and 'The Dog House' he mused, studying her every move while the mellow sounds of Louis Armstrong and Ella Fitzgerald played softly on the radio.

"So you want to get to know me better. Learn all about my deepest secrets and fantasies?" Mick inquired.

"I already know everything I have to, Mickey, but what about this bogus murder charge hanging over your head," she asked, attempting to get dressed again. "Aren't you worried about—you know—what you know and not being able to say anything... or tell anybody?"

"Does this mean you love me?" he asked.

"You bet my ass, it does," she replied, using one of his favourite lines. "I was raised that, 'life isn't measured by the number of breaths we take, but by the moments that take it away', and I knew it the first time you looked at me and took mine," she admitted. "The first time I laid eyes on you in that little coffee shop around the corner," said the brunette, visualizing the day, the hour, the moment, the second and the breath— or lack of it—that made the circumstance so memorable.

"Well not to fret, brown-eyes. I'll be around to take yours away for a long, long time to come and tomorrow's another day. So why don't you forget all about those nasty, outside distractions, get over here and climb aboard the Mickey-go-round? And let's just see if we can't create a breathtaking moment for the both of us."

"Why, Mr. Lannigan," she said, feigning a heavy, southern drawl. "I declare, you're insatiable. Why, I believe I have the *vapours*," she tittered, pretending to catch her breath.

Mick enjoyed her perfect smile as he tossed back the sheets from the bed and gazed at her with an inviting grin of his own.

"I can see you're going to be very demanding, and *very* hard to live with indeed, sir," she professed, staring back and seeing him embrace her full form with his baby blue, bedroom eyes.

"Better we leave that discussion for another time as well, darlin', and get down to what's really on your mind." He grinned, watching the teddy she was putting on slip and fall to the floor...